ADLER

ALAN BROWN

This is a work of fiction. Names, characters, places, and incidents are products of the author's imagination or are used fictitiously and are not to be construed as real. Any resemblance to actual events, locations, organizations, or persons, living or dead, is entirely coincidental.

World Castle Publishing, LLC
Pensacola, Florida
Copyright © Alan Brown 2021
Paperback ISBN: 9781953271723
eBook ISBN: 9781953271730
First Edition World Castle Publishing, LLC, February 22, 2021
http://www.worldcastlepublishing.com

Cover: Karen Fuller
Editor: Maxine Bringenberg

CHAPTER 1
THE BASEMENT

The dark was blinding. There were no windows. It was damp. It was cold. It was frightening.

The floorboards above him creaked — they were upstairs. But soon, they would be in the basement. He scanned the basement for exits and found three. The main exit that went from the first floor to the basement was the one they were certain to come down. The second exit was a freight elevator that spanned all three stories of the department store. He had used that freight elevator every night he worked to get the heavy floor waxing machine he used from one floor to another. That slow, aging elevator was loud. They would certainly hear it if he tried to escape in it. And, as slow as it was, they would likely be waiting for him when the door opened on another floor. That elevator would not be a viable way to escape.

That only left one option, that old hidden staircase in the back of the basement, concealed in a doorway in the rear of the alterations room. Years earlier, Adler employed dozens of talented dress and suit makers. The department where they worked was a large sewing and alterations room that occupied about half of the basement area — employees assigned to that department made dresses and custom suits. Adler employed several tailors that helped a customer select material, determine the style, and take measurements to custom fit the dress or suits, pants, and shirts. When the order was placed, the sewing and alterations department would go to work on designing the clothes. When the customer came back to the store to try on their clothes, the seamstress that did the work would use the secret stairway to bring the items up and place them in the back room that was contained on each floor. The tailor or salesclerk that sold the item would take it on the sales floor for the customer to inspect and try on. The seamstress would wait for the tailor or salesclerk to come back with any changes that needed to be made. In those days, a common worker was never allowed to enter the sales floor. They must always stay in the back room out of the view of the customers. If an item needed to be brought into the retail area, a sales associate would do that. That way, the common workers at Adler were always segregated from the store's well-heeled customers. The stairway existed on each of the floors in a back storage room, hidden from the shopping area of each floor.

In its prime, Adler was the premier department store in Kansas City, shopped by the wealthiest and most discriminating of Kansas City society. Customers were pampered. The wealthiest of them were treated like royalty. They had their own personal shopper employed by Adler to meet all their client's needs. They had their own shopping floor. That was the fourth floor. A special elevator, manned by a gentleman wearing a tuxedo, went to that floor. Only a small, select group of customers were invited to that floor, by appointment – only a select group of employees were permitted on that floor. The best sales associates, the best tailors, the best personal shoppers made that floor their home. Only one customer at a time was allowed on the fourth floor. Fine crystal chandeliers adorned the ceiling. Walls were covered with expensive paintings. Antique furniture, thick, soft carpet, and two fireplaces gave the room a look of a large parlor that one would expect to see in an elegant home. There were no racks of clothing, glass cases of fine jewelry, or any other indication that this was a sales floor in a department store.

When the customer exited the elevator, Linda Adler would be waiting to escort her customer to a sitting area. Hors d'oeuvres would be served, and a waiter would pour champagne or whatever beverage the customer preferred. When the customer was completely comfortable, models would begin walking out of the back room, one at a time, displaying the new fashions hand-selected by the customer's personal shopper. A tailor stood by to take measurements and correctly fit the clothing selections the customer made. A seamstress was summoned up to the back room of the fourth floor once the tailor had done his job. Typically, three appointments were scheduled on the fourth floor each day, six days a week. There would be a late morning appointment, a late afternoon, and an early evening appointment. Priority in setting the appointments was given to the customers that spent the most money.

In its heyday, an invitation to the fourth floor was an honor, a true recognition of one's wealth and status in the community. But those days were long ago. Old money customers had been replaced with new money customers. The times of living on one's opulence and relishing comforts that came with it had been replaced with a generation of society that had worked hard to earn their wealth and were determined not to waste it. They cared more about quality, value, and speed of delivery than they did about service.

With declining sales, increased competition, and costs of maintaining their own dress and suit making operation skyrocketing, Adler had been forced to shut down their sewing and alterations department twenty years earlier. The fourth floor remained open and used mainly for offices until a little over ten years ago. Both rooms remained unused, gathering dust and succumbing to age and neglect. The secret stairway that was used to connect the two areas also remained unused, neglected, and in deteriorating condition. The alterations room was now used for storage. The fourth floor had only its shell remaining. The antique furniture, crystal chandeliers, paintings, soft, thick carpeting, and all decorations had been removed, placed elsewhere in the store, sold, or destroyed. The room had been sealed off, and utilities going to the room had been turned off in an effort to cut costs. It was a ghost floor now, a floor the strangers that came into Adler that night wouldn't know about. It was a floor without surveillance cameras. It was a floor where he could hide and not be discovered. Connor had no idea if he could escape to that floor from the hidden stairway, but he would need to try.

When needed, that stairway would be his only way to escape. He had never used those stairs before—he didn't know if anyone had for many years. They might be unsafe. The doors leading out of the stairway on each floor might be locked or even sealed off. If they were, he would be trapped. But he couldn't worry about that. There was no other escape route out of the basement. He had no choice.

The stairs were on the other side of the basement, sixty yards from where Connor was hiding. He needed to move to them, but he had to be careful. It was dark, and he could only see a few inches in front of him. Dozens of mannequins surrounded him, lined up like rows of dominos. Bumping into one could start a chain reaction. Their hard, plastic bodies would make a loud noise colliding with the floor. The people upstairs would hear the noise—they would know where he was.

The basement at Adler was huge, just about the size of a football field. There were hundreds of places to hide. He had chosen to hide between the rows of life-size mannequins when he heard them coming down the stairs the first time. Connor was skinny like a pole. He was easily able to hide behind one of the larger male mannequins and not be spotted during their first inspection of the area. He was hiding there when the lights suddenly went out. He had not moved since. They were watching. They were listening. He had felt safe hidden amongst the life size mannequins. The time they came into the basement after they first arrived, they had not noticed him. But they weren't looking for him then. Old man Collins had told them he was the only person in the store. They believed him. After all, they had a gun pointed at his head.

Connor needed to escape sixty yards to the stairway. The entire path to it was covered with relics from the past, now obstacles to his escape. Any noise would alert the strangers. Without lights, without windows, visibility was limited to a foot or two. Connor's movements to the stairway would be based on memory of the obstacles in his path. He tried to remember. What was between him and the stairway? There were the mannequins, about two dozen along the path. There were the seasonal decorations. He didn't need to worry about the Christmas decorations — they were set up throughout the store. There were plenty of empty boxes, though. Then, there were plenty of other seasonal decorations stored in the basement — Easter, Halloween, Valentine's Day, Fourth of July, Mother's Day, Father's Day — all sitting in his path. Also stored away in the basement were the summer seasonal items, including sports equipment, camping equipment, and recreational merchandise. Nearly every inch of the basement floor was used for storage. It was a wonderful place to hide, but not a very good place to escape in a hurry in the dark.

The fourth floor would offer him the best opportunity to escape, alert someone, and hide until help came. The problem was that there was a minefield of merchandise that, if knocked over, would alert the strangers to his location, between him and that stairway. They had guns. He had nothing to protect himself. Even if he was able to take the stairway to the fourth floor, there was no way out once he got there. That rear stairway was the only way to travel between the floors. If they discovered that stairway, they could discover him.

***

Connor Allen had been in that basement dozens of times before, but not like this. Before, there were lights. Before, he was alone except for Old Man Collins. Bill Collins was the store security guard that worked the graveyard shift. He had worked at Adler for nearly ten years, ever since he retired from the Kansas City police force. He retired two weeks after his wife was diagnosed with cancer, which doctors had discovered too late. The cancer had spread throughout her body and into her lungs. There was nothing they could do for her. They had lost their only child, a son, five years earlier in Viet Nam. All they had was each other. Bill left the police force to spend as much time as possible with his wife. That turned out to be only three months. When she passed, he needed to keep busy to keep his mind from going crazy, so he applied to an advertisement that Adler ran in the *Kansas City Star* looking for a security guard. Linda Adler offered him a job.

The graveyard shift was lonely. Five nights a week, he was by himself. The sixth night, Connor worked. They talked. They took their lunch break together. Old Man Collins was like a grandfather to Connor, Connor like the son Bill Collins had lost in the war. They enjoyed each other's company. Connor talked about school, girlfriends, cross country, and track. Bill Collins liked to listen to him. They talked about the Royals and the Chiefs. Both were big fans, but football was the favorite sport for both of them. They talked about Len Dawson, the quarterback for Kansas City. He was a favorite customer of Adler and was their favorite football player. Connor had never met him — Bill Collins had. A week before Connor's seventeenth birthday, Old Man Collins got Len Dawson to sign a photograph of himself. Bill surprised Connor that Saturday night with the gift, framed and wrapped. Connor put it on his bedroom wall, where it had remained ever since.

Bill Collins spent most of the night in the security office in the basement. Three offices ran along the west wall of the basement. The first was Linda Adler's office, the largest of the three rooms. Nothing was out of place in her office. There wasn't a piece of paper on her desk. There wasn't a file out of place. Linda Adler ran her store like she ran her life. Everything was immaculate. Everything had a place and a purpose. She was disciplined, and so were her employees. Everyone followed the system and schedule that Linda Adler set up. There was no deviation. There were no mistakes. She was tough but fair. Everyone seemed to respect her, and everyone knew that when she said something, she meant it. Her office was a reflection of her. It was clean to the point of almost being sterile. You would think from looking inside that no one actually worked in that office. There were no visible signs of it being disturbed by inhabitants. There was not a speck of dust, a piece of trash, or even a scuff mark on the walls or floor.

The second office in the basement was the accounting office. The people in that office handled payroll, accounts receivable, and payables. They counted the money at night and prepared the cash registers for the morning. One employee of the accounting department, Virginia Lighter, was responsible for depositing the day's receipts in the safe every night. The safe, made of thick concrete, was embedded in the wall in the accounting office. Virginia was an elderly, white haired lady in her late sixties and had worked at Adler for nearly forty years. She was the only employee, other than Linda Adler, that had the combination to the safe. The next day, Linda Adler would take the money from the previous day's receipts and drive two blocks to the First National Bank. There, she would deposit the receipts into Adler's account.

The third office in the basement was the security room — that's where Bill Collins spent most of his evenings. The room had video screens that were fed pictures from a dozen video cameras strategically located throughout the store. It also showed feeds from cameras located at the entrances, exits, and around the dock area. Old Man Collins could view every floor and every key location within the store and leading into and out of the store.

Once an hour, he would do a walk-through on all three floors and the basement, just to make sure that everything was secure. Otherwise, he watched the security monitors in his room. That's where he was when he saw the strangers approaching the dock entrance to the first floor. Connor was less than twenty feet away, waxing the floor in Linda Adler's office when he darted past him heading upstairs. Connor knew something was wrong. He never knew Bill Collins to run anywhere. Connor turned off the floor wax machine and walked into the security office to see what had caused Bill to run upstairs.

***

That's when he saw four men enter the first floor through the dock entrance. Connor watched as Bill Collins approached the men. He saw a scuffle take place and saw Old Man Collins fall to the floor. They dragged him to the steps leading down to the basement. That's when Connor moved to a hiding place amongst the mannequins. The security guard was dragged down the steps to his office. One of the men put a gun to Bill's head. Connor overheard the man ask if anyone else was in the store. Bill said that he was alone. As the intruder held the barrel of the gun to the security guard's head, Bill begged for his life. Connor heard the shot but was too petrified to look. Connor watched, his body trembling with fear, as the intruder went to the breaker box next to Linda's office. One by one, the lights in the building turned off as the intruder flipped off the power from the breaker box. Soon the only remaining light came from the three offices in the basement. Connor watched as the building went dark.

One man was left behind in the basement to monitor the security cameras. Another went into the accounting office and began working to open the safe. The other two went upstairs to begin their search for valuables. One of the men that stayed downstairs opened the door to Linda's office. Connor was certain he would notice the floor waxing machine at the back of the office. If he did, the strangers would know that Bill Collins wasn't the only person in the store that night. But, the stranger didn't notice. He stuck his head inside the office and turned out the light, shutting the door behind him as he left. Then he shut the doors to the security room and the accounting office. With the office doors shut, the entire basement went dark.

Connor could not move for fear of being heard or seen. The two intruders that remained in the basement were only feet away from him. Even with the doors to the offices closed, any noise could alert them to his presence. He could hear his heart race and could feel the trembling of his body. Any second, his legs might give out, causing him to fall and alert the thieves. It was just too quiet. Why couldn't they make noise? Noise would drown out the beating of his heart, his heavy breathing, his movements. But the strangers in the basement were silent. He needed to sneeze. He needed to cough. His mouth was dry, and his throat tickled. His breathing was labored, and he could hear every breath he took. He was sure they could hear him. Any second, they would open their door and come looking for him.

Connor had been in the basement hundreds of times. He knew every inch of it and had always felt comfortable and safe there. The security guard had always been close, in his office at one side of the basement. If he had needed him, he could shout, and Bill would come running. He loved being in a place of forgotten years. He loved dreaming of the stories that could be told from the items living out their remaining life in that basement. The basement was a solemn, peaceful place to him. Most items in that basement had not been used in many years. They were remembrances of better times. They had retired to live out their remaining life in a cold, dark dungeon surrounded by other relics of a wonderous past. Before, he did not need to hide among the seasonal ornaments, decorations, and mannequins that were permanent residents of the basement at Adler Department Store. Before, they were like old friends, reminders of a slower pace of life. Now they were obstacles complicating his escape.

He could barely see a few feet in front of him. The only thing that was plainly visible was the white athletic shirt he was wearing, his favorite shirt. It had the University of Kansas logo on the front with the words "Track Team" embedded in deep blue lettering below. He'd received it as a gift from Coach Schmidt when he visited their campus a month earlier. Connor was hoping for an athletic scholarship, and he had visited several universities, but KU was the one he had dreamed of going to ever since he first started to be a serious runner. He had lived his whole life in the middle-class suburbs of Prairie Village, Kansas. He lived just a few blocks away from the state line and Kansas City, Missouri, but he had always considered himself a Kansas kid. He had been invited to visit the University of Missouri and their track program, but he never even considered going. Missouri was KU's biggest rival. The two schools hated each other. There was no way that he was going to be disloyal to the state he had grown up in. Besides, KU was the alma mater of great milers like Jim Thorpe, Jim Ryan, and Wes Santee. If he was going to run the mile in college, he was determined to be trained by the best program in the country.

He was damn proud of that T-shirt, but in hindsight, he wished he had chosen a darker, less noticeable shirt. He could easily be spotted in that shirt, even in the dark. So far, they had no idea that he was there. Bill had bought him time. He told his killers that no one else was in the store, and they seemed to have believed him. Maybe he would be safe if he just didn't move. They weren't looking for him. If they didn't come close, they would not spot him hiding amongst the mannequins. But what if they did come close? What if he sneezed or coughed or knocked over one of the mannequins? They would find him then. They had flashlights. Connor had seen them when the men first came into the basement. That would give them an advantage if they were to hunt for him. But Connor had an advantage they didn't. He knew his way around every part of that store. He had been working there for nearly two years. He had cleaned, waxed, and polished every inch of all three floors of that store once a week for twenty-three months.

How were the strangers able to enter the store? Connor thought to himself. Every door was locked. An alarm was hooked up to every entrance. Even when the janitorial staff arrived early in the morning, they would need to wait at the front door for Bill to turn off the alarm from his security room before entering the store. Then Connor realized something else he hadn't considered before. The alarm never went off when the strangers entered the store. Bill Collins did not turn off the alarm. The strangers must have disabled it somehow.

***

He remembered the first day he started working for Adler. His grandmother, Rose, had recommended him for the job. She had worked at the store for nearly twenty years but didn't need to work. Her husband was vice-president for a large, successful architectural firm in Kansas City and worked long hours. Grandma Rose liked to keep busy. She also liked shopping. Adler provided her the best of both worlds. She was able to work flexible hours that enabled her to keep busy, and she was able to see the new, seasonal inventory of fashionable clothes as soon as they came in before the regular shoppers saw them. The twenty-percent discount she received as an employee was an added incentive. Linda Adler let her employees charge their store purchases against their paychecks each month. Most months, Grandma Rose was in the "red" when the paychecks were passed out. She'd give the outstanding balances of her purchases to her husband, Ronald, and he'd pay whatever the difference was between his wife's paycheck and her shopping bill. He never complained. Fact was, her shopping cost him a whole lot less when she was working than it did before she started to work at Adler. At least now, part of her day was occupied with working, which meant less time shopping.

Grandma Rose spoke highly of Connor. He was young, only sixteen when he first went to work at Adler. "He is very responsible," she told Linda. "He's a hard worker, and he is dependable."

Linda decided to give Connor a chance. He would have a probationary period, six weeks. At the end of that period, she would decide if he would stay on. As with her other employees, Linda demanded perfection. Connor's only responsibility was to sweep and wax the floors throughout the store. He had eight hours to get the job done. But the floors had to look perfect— no dirt, no dust, no scuff marks would be tolerated. Every floor had to shine. She showed him exactly how to run the floor wax machine and showed him how she wanted the floors to look. He was scheduled to work only Saturday nights from ten to seven, with an hour for lunch. The store was closed on Sunday. The janitorial service would arrive at 7am Sunday morning, unlock the door and let him and Old Man Collins out. The doors were locked all night. Even Bill didn't have a key to the front door. He was told that in the event of an emergency, there was a key to the front door contained within a red box in Linda's desk drawer.

***

Adler was a large department store located in one of the nicest, wealthiest areas of Kansas City, the Plaza. It was like a small city's version of Bloomingdales. The store was a third generation, family owned. In its younger days, Martha Ellen Truman was a loyal customer. Her husband, President Harry Truman, used to call the owner, Thomas Adler, whenever he needed a special gift for his wife's birthdays, anniversaries, or Christmas. The president rarely had a clue what to get his wife. He left that up to Mr. Adler. The store maintained extensive files on all their best customers. They recorded sizes, styles, and a wish list of gifts based on the client's buying habits and taste. Mr. Adler would select a gift based on the monetary amount the president wanted to spend, gift wrap it, and ship the gift directly to the White House.

Adler was the department store of preference for governors, senators, congressmen, mayors, manufacturing moguls, CEOs, and their wives. Nearly everyone that was anyone in Kansas City society shopped at Adler. They were the first store in the Midwest to offer personal shopping to their best customers. Mary Adler, wife of Thomas Adler, heard about the service offered to the most well-heeled customers at several of the most prestigious stores in New York City. She traveled to see them and was so impressed by the service that she insisted her husband implement it at Adler. Thomas Adler resisted the idea at first, but with persistence, his wife was able to convince him to give it a try.

Personal shopping was an instant success and became a mainstay of Adler. The store offered the service to its best customers. The service was not only well-received by its customers, but it was also embraced by Adler employees. The commissions paid from self-generated sales were generous. Some salesclerks worked their entire lives at Adler, developing their own clientele. They maintained lists of the merchandise that their clients bought and were interested in buying. They made notes of birthdays, anniversaries, weddings, and graduation dates for their clients and their family members. They contacted their clients several days, or even weeks before an important date, and would offer suggestions for gifts. They also contacted their clients when new, seasonal arrivals were about to be delivered to the store. That gave them the first opportunity to pick before the items hit the shopping floors for the general public. The best of the best personal shoppers made it to the fourth floor. That was the crown jewel. To work on the fourth floor at Adler meant the ultimate success. Incomes were high, prestige was even higher. The clientele that was invited to the fourth floor were the cream of society. They were the wealthiest customers the store had. Employees of Adler that were successful enough to work on that floor made higher commissions than employees that worked on other floors.

A staple of the Adler shopping experience, personal shopping, had ended ten years earlier when Erma Schmidt retired. She had worked at Adler for forty-two-years and was the last of the sales clerks to provide personal shopping to her clients. At one time, she had over two-hundred customers on her personal client list. Commissions from her sales made Erma a very good living. The last few years, her client list had dropped to a mere handful of customers. Most of them were older customers, holding on to the traditions of the past. The concept of personal shopping was lost on the younger generation. Commission sales, which had been the life blood for Adler's salesclerks years earlier and was a great motivator for them to provide personal shopping, had ended a decade earlier. Today's salesclerks worked on a base salary with a bonus tied to achieving pre-determined sales goals. The new generation compensation fed mediocrity in sales performance. Salesclerks today were mere order takers. They had little incentive to go after sales because they were compensated exactly the same for waiting for the customer to come to them.

The glory days of Adler were gone. Prestigious people no longer sought the store out for their shopping needs. There were plenty of newer, quality department stores to choose from. Many were located in malls, which offered a variety of stores and restaurants to choose from to enhance their shopping experience. Adler was a dinosaur. It was a relic. It was dying, but it was a slow death — it had been dying for years. Its building was old. Repairs were expensive. Sales were falling. Costs were increasing, and revenue was dropping.

The grandeur of the Plaza area of Kansas City had kept locals and visitors coming back to the area despite the mass exodus of people to the suburbs, and consequently to the malls and shopping areas in their respective markets. The Plaza had kept Adler Department Store on life support for many years. Finally, Linda Adler had decided to pull the plug. She had announced that, after sixty-two-years of operation, Adler would close after the first of the year. This would be its final Christmas season. Her announcement was made the day after Thanksgiving during the Christmas lighting ceremony in the Plaza.

In a fitting tribute to the death of an institution of Kansas City, storm clouds came over Kansas City that evening, and a downpour shortened the beginning of the Christmas shopping season celebration.

Crowds flocked to Adler that Christmas season. Some had never been in the store before and were curious. Visitors marveled at the elaborate themed Christmas displays that sat inside the windows that ran along the front of Adler's first floor along Grand Avenue. Crowds gathered outside the windows to watch the displays. Each had a different Christmas theme and was created by local artists. Many of those artists had created store front displays for Adler in past years and wanted to leave their mark on the last Christmas season at Adler. One artist even used live actors to re-create a windowfront scene from the movie *It's a Wonderful Life*. Parents and grandparents all had stories to tell about experiences they'd had in the store. Past customers that had not been in Adler for years came back for one last shopping experience. Families, some bringing several generations of relatives, shopped together. Everyone wanted to buy something from Adler. Everyone wanted to create one last memory. Their last Christmas season was the best for Adler in nearly thirty years.

***

It was those huge sales and the thought of a large payout that brought those four strangers to Adler late that Saturday night. Each had been in the store many times before that night, not to shop, but to observe. The men observed each location of the video surveillance cameras. One took note of items of particular value in the jewelry department. Another was tasked with taking inventory of the fur coats and high-end clothes. A third man observed the display cases that held fine crystal. They watched at night to observe the security that was present when everyone else went home. One observed Old Man Collins making his hourly rounds. Another observed Linda Adler making her bank deposits. They knew that Linda Adler made those bank deposits every morning. That meant the day's receipts stayed in the store overnight. The group picked the night of the busiest shopping day of the year, December 23, two days before Christmas, and the last shopping day until after Christmas, to invade the store. Adler was always closed on Sunday. A city ordinance at the time prohibited retail stores from doing business on Sundays. Adler would keep their sales receipts in the store, in the safe, until December 26.

The date was set to rob the store—Saturday, December 23, late at night. The security guard never had a chance. His fate was sealed the day the robbery was planned. The strangers didn't try to disguise themselves. They didn't wear ski masks. Bill Collins got a good look at them from the surveillance camera posted at the rear entrance by the dock. They were young.

***

Connor got a look at them too. They looked to be about his age, maybe a little older. They didn't look like a street gang. They all had short hair, and none had beards, visible tattoos, earrings, or flashy gold or silver jewelry that Connor associated with gang members. They looked like regular teenagers. Then, it hit him. He was sure he had seen one of the strangers before. The leader, the one that held the gun to Bill's head and pulled the trigger, was someone Connor knew. He couldn't remember his name or where he'd seen him, but Connor was certain he recognized the man.

CHAPTER 2
IN THE SHADOW OF THE MANNEQUINS

Connor was just about to move toward the rear stairway when the door to the security room opened. A young man — white, with short brown hair, glasses, a thin face wearing jeans, a blue tee-shirt, and tennis shoes — emerged from the office. The stranger turned out the light to the room, shut the door behind him, and walked upstairs. Connor listened for the sound of his footsteps to go away. Now, there was only one stranger in the basement, the man in the accounting office. That door was still shut, a ray of light shooting out of the opening between the bottom of the door and the floor. There was a muffled sound coming from the room — it sounded like a drill. *The safe,* Connor thought to himself. *That room has the safe with the day's deposits. The stranger is breaking into it. He will be gone as soon as he gets into that safe and takes whatever is inside. Then, all four of them will leave the store.* He would be safe. That's what he thought.

There would be no need to get to the back stairway, Connor reasoned. Bill had told them that no one else was in the store. They had no reason to think otherwise. All he needed to do was keep quiet and out-of-sight until they left. He scanned the area around him, looking for a better hiding place. His eyes were adjusting to the dark, so he could see better now. The mannequins that surrounded him shielded him from being easily spotted. But he was only about twenty feet from the accounting office and about sixty feet from the stairs leading up to the first floor. That was closer than he wanted to be to the intruders. His white shirt worried him. He was concerned that someone would spot it with its contrast to the darkness surrounding him. If he was spotted and he needed to escape to that hidden stairway, it would be better if he had more distance between him and the intruders.

Connor decided to move, slowly, quietly, carefully toward the alterations room and the back stairway. The shelves containing seasonal decorations were located just twenty feet deeper into the basement. The Christmas decorations were gone, but empty boxes remained, and other seasonal decorations would shield him from sight. Three rows of shelving contained the decorations. Each row was approximately eighteen-feet wide, containing three-racks in each row and four shelves per rack. Each row of shelving was about ten feet high. He set his target on moving to the area behind the third row of shelving. It was about fifty feet from the office area and directly in front of the alterations room. They could not spot him there unless they walked to the other end of the basement. That area would be a safe place to wait until the strangers left. He took five steps toward the shelving, and his body froze. He was trembling. His legs were dragging behind his body. They refused to move any farther. He would wait there for a minute or so for his trembling to slow.

***

Waxing floors at Adler was hard work. There were three stories of floors, each about a football field in length and nearly the same distance in depth. All the floors were made of fine cherry wood. The beauty salon was the only exception. It was located on the first floor and had a linoleum floor. In addition to the three stories, there were the three offices in the basement. Before any of the floors could be waxed, rugs that covered several areas of the floor had to be removed. Then, every inch of the floors had to be swept.

The broom, dustpan, and floor waxing machine were

kept in the basement in the janitor's closet at the far back of the basement. That was where Connor would start every Saturday night. He would sweep the offices in the basement, then move to the first floor, second, and the third floor. Once he was done sweeping, he would start the process over again in the basement, this time waxing the floors.

When he'd first started working at Adler, he dreaded using the floor wax machine. It was heavy, weighing nearly as much as he did. It was hard to control. When he first turned it on, the machine seemed to have a mind of its own. It jumped. It moved. It took Connor in whatever direction it decided to go. It took all his strength to control that machine. The vibration in its handles numbed his hands and arms after a while. He could only wax for a few minutes before he would need to take a short break—sweep a little, wax a little, then sweep a little. Connor found it very difficult to get the entire store swept and waxed in the nine hours he was allotted. He skipped lunches most nights to work through them. Connor was determined to get the job done well and on time. Ms. Adler told him that it could be done. She set the bar high for him, and he was determined to clear it. Connor was not a quitter. He refused to give up.

That's what made him such a good athlete, such a good long-distance runner. He refused to quit. During the winter of his junior year at Shawnee Mission East High School, he was training for the Kansas State Indoor Championship. He had already qualified for the mile and half-mile race, but bettering the two-mile qualifying time of nine minutes and forty-five seconds had eluded him. Four times he had broken ten-minutes, once running a nine-forty-eight, just three seconds from qualifying. Most athletes would be satisfied with qualifying for two races at the state meet, but not Connor. It was a matter of pride. He was a talented long-distance runner, finishing fifth in the state Cross Country Championship the previous fall. He knew he could break nine-forty-five for a two-mile race.

He had one opportunity left to qualify, an invitational track meet at Pittsburg State University in Pittsburg, KS. Coach Englund, the Shawnee Mission East track coach, had only entered Connor in the two-mile race at that invitational. That way, he would be well-rested for the race. Connor's workouts leading up to the race were encouraging. He had broken his body down earlier in the year with long, slow distance workouts. Two weeks earlier, Coach Englund had started combining interval workouts with the distance workouts. Connor had built up his endurance and now was working on building his speed.

Indoor races were much different than outdoor races. The main difference was the oval track that the races were run on. They were considerably shorter and rounder than outdoor tracks. It normally took ten laps to equal a mile on an indoor track. It would take only four laps to equal a mile on an outdoor track.

Consequently, the indoor tracks were rounded, with sharper, more frequent turns. There was no advantage of a long straightaway to relax and make a move on a lead runner. You were constantly turning on an indoor track. To pass someone, you would need to go high on the oval to get around them — that added distance to your run.

The grip of the track was different too. Outdoor tracks were primarily cinder. Runners would wear spikes on their shoes to dig into the surface of the track. On rainy days, a runner would use extra-long spikes to gain better traction. Those spiked shoes grabbed hold of the track like racing tires on a sports car. But the indoor tracks were like running on a rug. Spikes were useless. An athlete would have to rely on his regular running shoes. In a long race like the two-mile, a runner's legs would sweat. That sweat would roll down to the shoes. The shoes would become wet and would slide on the surface of the track. A runner just didn't have as much control on an indoor track as they did on an outdoor track. Injuries were more likely too. Friction caused from the track's surface colliding with wet shoes and feet caused blisters and foot ailments. Sliding of feet caused the body to jerk, which caused leg and back problems. Twisted ankles, blood blisters, chin splints, and leg cramps were common ailments.

Two days before the indoor meet, Connor started to get a cold. That wasn't unusual—it happened almost every February. The combination of harsh Kansas City winters and overtraining were the culprits that brought on a cold. It was no big deal. Connor had run many races while suffering from a cold. This time of year, it could take him two weeks or longer to get over one. He wasn't going to let that interfere with his track season. But the night before the track meet, the cold went into his chest, making it painful to breathe. This cold was different, more intense than any he had before. But it wasn't going to stop him. This was his last chance to qualify for the state two-mile. He barely got any sleep the night before. He downed aspirin and cough drops on the trip down to Pittsburg State, right up until it was time to warm-up for the two-mile race. It was the final event of the track meet, scheduled to be run at eight in the evening, but was running over an hour behind. Connor had been sitting around all day. He drank plenty of water to stay hydrated, and he chewed on aspirin and cough drops throughout the day and evening. He couldn't talk—it was too painful. He hadn't been able to eat anything all day. He stretched and warmed-up for nearly an hour before the race and worked up a good sweat by the time the runners lined up at the starting line.

When the starter's gun went off, Connor moved to the front of the pack. This wasn't his normal race strategy. He preferred the strategy that Jim Ryan had used for so many years with great success. That strategy called for him to hang back in the pack—to stay within striking distance of the lead runner, but far enough back that he could be shielded from the wind. Even indoors, the area directly behind another runner created a sort of vacuum in which motion felt less taxing. The other advantage of staying behind the lead runners was that he could see them struggle. He would watch for a change in their gate. He would watch for their arms to stray away from their body. Those were indications of exhaustion. That was when he would make his move.

In this race, however, Connor decided to go to the front of the pack on the very first lap. He had never done that before, but he had never felt this bad in a race before. He needed immediate separation from the pack. They were like wolves hunting their prey. If he stayed within the pack, they would hear his labored breathing and see the pain in his face. Once they sensed his weakness, the race would be over. Distance running was as much about mental toughness as it was about physical toughness. He would not have a chance. Every runner in that pack had trained just as hard as he had. Every runner in that race was just as fast and had just as much endurance as he had. The difference between him and them was mental toughness. If they sensed his physical weakness, no amount of mental toughness could overcome their confidence in beating a wounded runner.

At the halfway mark, Connor was thirty yards ahead of the next runner. He clocked a four-thirty-two mile, over twenty-seconds under the pace he needed to maintain to qualify for State. With two laps left, three runners caught him. His pace had slowed. He was running on fumes. His body had given out a lap earlier, but Connor refused to let anyone pass him, and he refused to give up. Connor shortened his stride, lifted his legs, quickened his steps. His arms that had wandered to his side showed new life. He pulled them into his ribs, opened his hands, and pointed his thumbs directly in front of him. As his pace quickened, the motion of his arms quickened. His mouth opened wide to suck every bit of air into his lungs. Connor straightened his body directly over his legs. Then suddenly, he let out a loud cry and willed his body to leave everything it had on that track.

The crowd came alive for the final lap. Four runners were within inches of each other, with only one trip around that short oval remaining. Less than three feet separated Connor from the other three runners. Connor clung to the inside line of the track. If anyone was going to beat him, they would need to go to the outside to do it. They would need to run a farther distance to win the race. His feet had gone numb—he could not feel them touching the track. His heart was racing. Staring straight ahead, his sole focus was on the finish line. So when he broke the tape at the finish line, he did not hear the crowd cheer or see the race clock. Connor knew he had won the race when he felt the tape break as he crossed the finish line, but he was blinded by the sweat that blanketed his eyes. Within seconds, he felt dizzy and fell to the track, losing consciousness.

A medical crew raced to his side. An ambulance rushed him to the nearest hospital, Hawthorne Medical Center. Connor did not wake up for nearly two days. When he did, he learned that his cold had penetrated his chest and had caused inflammation around his heart. He nearly died from that cold. Connor's finish time for that race did qualify him for the state meet, but he would never run it. Instead, he spent the next several weeks in the hospital, and when he was finally released, Connor was far too weak to continue running, at least for the remainder of that season. He missed the rest of the track season and lost his chance for a college scholarship. Connor would never attend the University of Kansas.

It took a month before Connor could control that floor wax machine. By then, his hands had become used to the vibration, and no longer went numb. At that point, he worked on the fastest, most efficient way to get his job done. He determined that sweeping all three floors and the basement offices first and then operating the floor wax machine after was the most efficient use of his time. When he finished sweeping the floors, he would start the floor wax machine in the basement offices. After finishing them, he would take a lunch break, normally with Bill. After lunch, he would take the old freight elevator to the first floor, wax it, then move to the second floor, and finally the third floor. With time, he became fast enough and efficient enough that he would normally finish his work with an hour or so to spare. He would watch the sunrise from the big glass windows on the first floor.

Then, he would explore. Adler was a fascinating place. With the sun starting to come through those big, glass windows, it wasn't a frightening place like it sometimes appeared in the middle of the night. At night, he sometimes imagined ghosts or strangers hiding in the store. The floors creaked. The old furnace in the basement made noises running through the vents. Shadows appeared out of nowhere from the headlights of cars driving down the street. Every noise was amplified in the still of the night. On stormy nights, the wind ripped through the ceiling above the fourth floor, causing sounds that echoed through the building walls. All those noises were frightening to him when he first started working at Adler. But he took comfort in knowing that Bill was there in the basement, in his security room, watching the video monitors, watching out for Connor.

But tonight, Bill could not help him. He was alone. Those frightening noises were real. The nightmares he had those first few weeks at Adler had come true, and they were worse than anything he had imagined.

The times he explored that old building after his work was done had led to the discovery of that hidden stairway. It was Bill that had told him where it went. It was Bill that told him about the fourth floor. Neither had been up those stairs. Once, a few weeks earlier, Connor was determined to go up them. He had heard many stories from his grandmother about the glory days of that floor and was curious about what it was like up there. He was curious why that floor had been sealed off and not used for so many years. Bill told him that the floor was closed and sealed off after a murder-suicide took place on that floor. Connor had never heard that story before. He wasn't even sure if the story was true.

It could have just been a story that Old Man Collins made up to keep Connor from exploring. He had always assumed the floor was closed because of declining sales and to keep utility costs down. That's what he had heard.

But after hearing Bill's story about the murder, he decided to research it in the city library. There was nothing about the murder-suicide listed in the *Kansas City Star* papers around the date of the murder. Connor confronted Bill with that news. He said it was all part of a cover-up. Old Man Collins knew the real reason why that floor was closed. He was a policeman on the Kansas City police force when the murder occurred.

According to him, it was quite a scandal and an even better cover-up. Ms. Adler had married a man by the name of David Morgan thirty-years ago. Back then, she went by the name Linda Adler-Morgan. She had just inherited the family business from her father, Thomas Adler, who had passed from a heart attack two months earlier. Linda's mother had died in a car accident ten years earlier. She was an only child and so became the sole beneficiary of her father's estate. She inherited the store in its prime. In addition, she inherited the mansion in Leawood that had been in her family for three generations. Then, there were the stocks that her father had invested in months after the stock market crash of '29. While others sold, he bought. He had accumulated a great deal of wealth from those stock investments. Now, it all belonged to Linda. Overnight, she had become a wealthy woman.

She met David Morgan at a charity event she hosted. He was tall, handsome, good-looking, and very charismatic. He came from a slightly lower social class than Linda, but that didn't matter to her. She fell for his charm almost immediately. They dated for less than a month before he proposed and married six months later. It was after they married that she discovered her husband was a man with many addictions. He was addicted to scotch. He was addicted to gambling. He was addicted to women.

One thing that he wasn't addicted to was work. He played until the sun rose. Then he slept until late afternoon and started the cycle again. He never tried to find a job. He burned through his wife's money like a fire in a lumber yard.

Whatever he didn't spend on fine, single malt scotch or horse racing and the blackjack table, he would spend in pursuit of women. He chased any young, thin, good looking woman he came across. It didn't matter if they were married or single. It didn't matter if they were friends of his wife or not. It didn't matter how indiscreet his affairs were. He just didn't care if his wife found out about the affairs.

His last sexual escapade took place on the fourth floor of Adler at three on a Sunday morning. His trophy was a young salesclerk at Adler, Denise Caldwell. She was an attractive twenty-two-year-old blonde, with long flowing hair, blue eyes, and a dark complexion, married to a much older man. He was wealthy — she had married him because of that. He also worked long hours, and she was lonely and vulnerable. She had never seen the fourth floor before. David offered her the opportunity to see it. He met her at the front door of Adler at eleven that night. Her husband was out of town on a business trip and was not expected back that night. David took her in the elevator to the fourth floor, where he had a bottle of chilled champagne waiting at a table next to the fireplace. They drank and kissed and got undressed.

Neither of them heard the noise of the elevator as it ascended to the fourth floor. They had their backs to it as the man exited. He approached the couple as they reached the climax of their passion. David saw the man as he raised a gun in his right hand. He leaped off his prey and sprinted toward the back room but heard the gunshot as it whizzed by his head. He heard the second gunshot as it struck a table a foot away from him. He dove and got behind a counter as he heard the screams of the woman he had been caught with, then a third and a fourth gunshot. Her screams went silent. On his hands and knees, he moved quickly into the back room. It was dark. The gunshots had stopped. It was eerily quiet. Suddenly, one more shot rang out. Then, total silence.

Speculation that the fourth floor was haunted by the ghosts of the people that died that night had kept Connor from going up those steps. Employees working the third floor at night had heard noises coming from above them on numerous occasions. Some had heard laughter. Others had heard cries. Most had heard screams. Several had heard a gunshot. That floor was never used again. Two weeks after the murders, everything was moved off that floor. A week after that, the elevator leading up to it was closed. The floor was sealed off from the rest of the building, not to be used again.

Connor had gotten up the nerve to open the door leading up that rear stairway a few weeks earlier. He had finished his work early, and curiosity got the best of him. He just had to see that fourth floor. The door leading up to it was blocked by empty shelving. He moved the clutter and opened the door. It was completely dark on the other side. He took two steps inside and walked right into several spider webs dangling down from the ceiling. Connor looked for a light switch, but there wasn't one. He pulled out the flashlight he had put in his pocket five minutes earlier, turned it on, and shined the light directly in front of him. It illuminated his path just enough to see a man on the staircase, ten feet in front of him. He dropped the flashlight and ran out the door, slamming it behind him. He had not opened the door since. Nor had he retrieved the flashlight he dropped in his hasty exit.

Connor didn't want to try to go up that stairway again. He didn't think he would need to. There was only one stranger left in the basement, and he had been in the accounting office for about twenty minutes. Surely he was close to opening that safe. Once he did, he would remove the money, turn out the light in the office, and leave. That was what Connor thought. Once he had the money and the other strangers had the valuables they were looking for, they would all leave the same way they had come in, by the shipping door at the rear of the first floor. Once they were gone, Connor could check on Bill. Maybe he was still alive. Maybe he could get help to him in time. Once the men were gone, he could call the police. Everything would be fine. He would be safe.

Now, he just needed to be concerned about the one man in the office twenty feet away from him. Connor was visible from that distance. It was time for him to move to a better hiding place, between the racks of seasonal material between him and the alterations room. Connor slowly stepped out from behind the mannequin, watching the accounting office door with one eye and the path in front of him with the other. He moved cautiously between the mannequins lined up like dominos around him. Fifteen feet to the first row of shelving. So far, so good. His body was trembling, his legs shaking from standing in place for twenty minutes. That was nothing to him. But this time, he stood in complete and overwhelming fear. His legs had locked up. They were difficult to move. It felt like the weight of his entire body, 152-pounds, had fallen to the area between his knees and ankles. His legs were heavy. He nearly had to drag them to move forward. With each movement, his body leaned forward, and his legs scooted the floor behind. It was as if heavy concrete blocks were tied to his ankles. Ten feet away, he saw the light in the office turn off. Connor was clearly visible now as he moved past the row of mannequins and was in an open area between them and the seasonal decorations. Connor had no choice. He had to run the last few feet to get between the first two rows of shelving. So, he took a deep breath, lifted his legs, and moved as quickly as possible.

He had just gotten behind the first row of shelving when the stranger walked out of the accounting office carrying a black duffle bag. Connor moved one more step to his right to take a position directly behind a large box on the shelf in front of him. That's when he felt it—the nail penetrating his running shoe and lodged in his left foot. The pain was intense. Connor did everything he could not to scream. He lifted his injured foot to remove the nail. That's when he lost his balance and fell into the large box directly in front of him. The crash made a sound—the stranger heard it. The intruder dropped his duffle bag, pulled out a gun, and walked toward Connor.

CHAPTER 3
BLOOD ON THE FLOOR

Connor pulled the nail out of his foot and watched as the stranger walked toward him. Forty feet away. Thirty feet away. He was coming directly toward Connor, directly toward the sound he had heard. Connor could not run. The pain in his foot was intense. He looked around for any possible hiding place. There were two large boxes in front of him on the bottom shelf. He quietly moved one to the right, the other to the left. He crouched in between the two, moving them as close to him as possible to hide. The area was dark. Perhaps he would not be visible.

Then he saw the flashlight—the stranger had a flashlight illuminating the seasonal boxes on the shelves ten-feet away from him. If the flashlight focused on him, he would surely be spotted. Damn that white running shirt he was wearing. It would be easy to see him. Connor reached around the shelving for anything he could use to protect himself in case he was spotted. Then he saw it. A box cutter was laying on the shelf above him. A storeroom employee must have left it there. There was a small opening at the back of the shelf, just an inch or so from the box cutter. He tried to reach his finger through the opening. It wouldn't fit. The stranger was ten feet away. The light from the flashlight was even closer. He looked for something thinner than his finger to reach through the opening in the shelf to pull down the box cutter. The only thing he could find was the nail he had pulled out of his foot. It had bent slightly when he stepped on it. He bent it, even more, making it into an L shape. He lifted it through the small opening and could feel the box cutter. He had one chance to get it. He lifted the nail just slightly and moved it to the other edge of the box cutter. Perhaps he could move it toward the opening, then lift it slightly so his finger could reach it.

Then he stopped all movement. The stranger was directly in front of him. Connor had run out of time. The man's flashlight was pointed at the fresh blood on the concrete floor in front of his hiding place. One drop of blood had fallen on the floor when he removed that nail. Connor had not noticed it. It must have fallen from the tip of the nail that penetrated his foot. The flashlight was focused on that drop of blood. Then he saw the stranger's hand drop down to touch it. The stranger raised the flashlight to Connor's hiding place. He would be discovered any second now.

There was only one other time in his life that he had been this frightened. He was hiding in the dark then too. He was six years old, and the school bus had just dropped him off. He remembered hearing the sirens in the distance. He walked one block to his house. His mother worked — she would not be home for another hour. His dad was also at work — he would not be home until supper time. For an hour, Connor would be alone in the house. He was used to it. He would turn on the television and watch cartoons. His mother had given him instructions not to play outside, not to open the door for anyone, not to answer the phone until she got home. His mother was protective. The neighborhood was safe. There was probably no reason to be concerned. But she couldn't help but worry about her only child.

He stood at the door and reached for the house key that was tied around his neck. He entered it in the lock and turned the doorknob. The sirens were louder now, closer. Connor opened the door and walked inside. There was a thin layer of smoke pouring into the living room from the basement door a few feet away. He flipped the light switch next to the front door. It did not turn on. He could smell smoke. He should have turned around and left the house, but those weren't the instructions his mother had given. "Remain in the house. Do not go outside," he remembered her saying. He tried to turn on the television. It wouldn't go on. He walked toward his bedroom. He would read until his mother came home, he decided.

Smoke had accumulated in the hallway leading to his bedroom, making it difficult to see. He touched the wall to help guide him. It was warm. When he reached his bedroom, the smoke had caused a haze that looked like fog occupying his room. Connor began to cough. The smoke was itching his throat and making it hard to breathe. He closed his bedroom door, hoping to keep the smoke out of his room.

The sirens were close, just down the street. Then he heard a loud noise, an explosion. He felt the temperature around him heat up. He saw the bright orange ambers of light shooting up from under his bedroom door. The house was on fire — he knew it now. The air was getting heavy. Connor grabbed the teddy bear that was resting on his pillow. He reached underneath the pillow and pulled out an old, faded medal. Then he pulled his special blanket off the bed. His mother had given him that blue blanket when he was a baby. He held it tightly every night when he went to sleep. It gave him comfort, made him feel safe. It protected him. He laid down on the floor underneath his bed and placed the medal around his neck. He held the teddy bear with one hand and the blanket with his other. He would often hide under the bed when he had a nightmare in the middle of the night. It was a safe place. He pulled the blanket on top of him, hiding himself and his teddy bear from the nightmare that was happening around him. His body was frozen with fear. Then there was a feeling of peace, a feeling that everything was going to be all right. He fell asleep.

A fireman heard a cry for help. He broke through the bedroom window and found Connor's lifeless body under the bed. He was not breathing — he was dead. But they would bring him back to life. During those few seconds between life and death, Connor would swear he talked to his grandpa. He would claim his grandfather told him to scream. He would claim his grandfather brought him back to the bedroom, his hiding place underneath the bed. He would claim his grandfather told him that he needed to go back home, that he could not stay with him. What Connor said about his grandfather would be dismissed as a dream. After all, his grandfather had died nearly six months earlier.

Connor was not ready to die this time either. As the stranger shined his flashlight on him, he had a split second to react before the stranger shot him. He reached one last time for the box cutter. He couldn't grab it. He leaped out of the shelving area that was hiding him. Out of pure survival instinct, he raised his left hand, which contained the bloodied nail. With all his force, Connor tightened his fist and jabbed the nail directly into the stranger's neck. Blood shot out of a vein on the side of his neck. The stranger stumbled backwards two steps and fell to the floor. The gun he was holding with one hand fell out of his grasp. The flashlight he was holding with the other hand rolled under the shelving. The flashlight and the gun made loud noises when they collided with the concrete floor. The stranger's body did not. He made a gurgling sound just after the nail penetrated his neck, but that sound went away in a few seconds. After that, he was completely silent. He landed on his back, his eyes open, staring at the ceiling, motionless. Connor looked at him for only a second, then he turned his head. He was a young man, not much older than Connor.

Connor picked up the gun and tried to reach for the flashlight. It was too far underneath the bottom of the shelving. He waited for a few seconds, listening for footsteps, hoping that the noise did not alert the other strangers on the first floor. He did not hear anyone. Connor thought about running for the hidden stairway. Then he thought about Bill Collins. Maybe he was still alive. They had left him in the security room — there was a phone in there. He could call for help. He could check on Old Man Collins and call for help. One thing was sure — the strangers would soon come downstairs to the basement to look for their friend. They would not leave without him. They would not leave without the money from the safe. When they discovered he wasn't in the accounting office, they would look for him. When they discovered his body, they would know that Connor was in the building. They could not leave a witness. They would search for him. He needed to buy as much time as possible. He needed some insurance, some reason for the strangers to keep him alive if they found him.

Connor moved quietly toward the offices. Every step on his left foot was painful. That nail must have gone in nearly an inch. Blood had coated his sock and was seeping into his shoe. He needed to take care of that wound. But not now — there wasn't time. He listened for the sounds of the men upstairs as he slowly made his way to the security room. If they started to come downstairs, he would need to run to that rear stairway.

When he got to the security office, the door was shut, the light off. He slowly opened the door. It was completely quiet. If Bill Collins was in there, he wasn't making a sound. Connor could only see a few inches in front of him in the dark of that office. The security monitors were dark. He couldn't turn on a light — that might be noticed. He moved slowly to the desk that sat in front of the row of video monitors. Bill and Connor often took their lunch break at that desk. The phone was near the right front corner of the desk. Connor picked up the receiver. There was no dial tone. The phone line must have been cut.

He moved to the closed closet at the back of the office. If Bill Collins was in that room, he must be in the closet. There was no other place to look. He opened the door slowly, afraid of what he would find behind it. On the floor of the closet lay Old Man Collins, dried blood on the left side of his head. His eyes were closed—he was motionless. Connor leaned over and shook his friend. His eyes suddenly opened, wide, large, almost bulging toward him. Bill Collins reached up with his left hand and motioned for Connor to come close. He wanted to tell him something.

"What is it, Mr. Collins?"

In a soft, strained voice, he said, "Get the key. It is the only way out."

The look he saw on the face of his friend almost knocked him over with fear. It was a look of death to come. He didn't utter another word. His eyes said everything. Connor could see the life draining out of his eyes. His friend was dying, and there was nothing he could do. He whispered to him that he would get help, to hang on. It wouldn't be long. Then Bill Collins's eyes closed. Connor shut the closet door and walked out of the office. Even if Connor survived the night and was able to get help for his friend, it would be too late. He knew it.

What did he mean when he said get the key? Connor wondered. Then he remembered what Bill Collins had told him before. "The key opens the doors." The key was his way out.

Connor went into Linda Adler's office. The key was supposed to be in her desk, inside a red box. He quietly checked every drawer. One drawer was locked. He used a letter opener that was lying on the desk to wedge the drawer open. It took a few minutes, but finally, he was able to pry it open. Inside the drawer was a red jewelry box. He opened it up, but the box was empty. The key was gone.

Connor needed to buy time. The sun would be coming over the horizon in about four hours. He needed to evade the strangers until then. They would surely leave before the sun came up. The janitorial crew would arrive at seven. The strangers would need to be gone before they arrived.

Connor moved to the accounting office. The door was shut. The man that found him must have shut the door before he started his search. Connor opened it and went inside, closing the door behind him. The safe was open, but there was nothing inside it. The filing cabinets had all been opened, and their contents were thrown on the floor. The entire floor was covered in papers and file folders. On top of the pile lay the black duffle bag the stranger had carried into the office—it was completely full. Inside were the contents of the safe, including the cash from the day's receipts. There must have been several thousands of dollars in that bag, along with checks and credit card receipts. Connor closed the bag, picked it up, and walked out of the office, closing the door behind him.

Connor's only plan was to take the hidden stairway to the fourth floor. He would hide the bag there and look for any way to escape or alert someone. First, he would hide the stranger's body. The longer it took his friends to find the body, the more time it bought Connor. Four hours. He just needed to hide out for four hours until daylight.

He moved quickly but carefully to the shelves that housed the seasonal decorations. It was pitch black. His eyes had adjusted somewhat to the dark, but still, he could only see a few feet in front of him. Damn, if he had only been able to reach that flashlight. He could really use it now and for that trip up the stairway. As he moved closer, he listened for footsteps. The strangers would come down the stairs from the first floor. If he listened carefully, he would hear them walking. But the deeper he got into the basement, the farther away those stairs were, the quieter their footsteps would be. He had to pay close attention to any noise. But the noise that he heard the loudest was the racing of his heart. He was more frightened than he had ever been, and he sure as hell wasn't looking forward to moving a dead body.

Before that night, Connor had only seen one dead body his entire life. That was his grandfather, at Newcomer Funeral Home. He remembered how afraid he was of going up to the casket. His mother told him that he didn't need to go. There was nothing to see. It was a closed casket. Grandma wanted it that way. But Connor knew he needed to go so he could say goodbye. His grandfather had been a mentor to him. The old man believed in him when no one else seemed to. Connor would have never become a runner if it wasn't for his grandfather's encouragement. His grandfather saw something inside him that no one else did. He saw the same competitive spirit that had made his grandfather so successful, and he saw a strong-willed youth that refused to give up. His grandfather was the one that encouraged Connor to run. He saw a restlessness inside his grandson that needed an outlet. So, his grandfather began running with Connor when he was four years old. They often ran from his house to the high school, ran around the track several times, and ran back home. Those times they ran together bonded them.

One Saturday, when he had finished running, his grandfather brought him into the house. He took Connor down to the basement and pulled out a dusty old shoe box from one of the shelves. Inside, the box was full of old medals. That day, his grandfather told him about his running days. Many years ago, his grandfather was a long-distance runner on the University of Kansas track team. In his youth, he had even qualified for the 1948 U.S. Olympic trials. In the finals of that meet, he finished fifth in the mile race that determined that year's Olympic athletes. After college, he ran several marathons and won a lot of races. In Connor's mind, his grandfather was a hero, and he wanted to be just like him. So, at the age of four, he decided that he was going to be a runner. Before his grandfather closed the box, he pulled out one medal and handed it to Connor—it was the first medal his grandfather had ever won. He told him to hold on to it, to keep it with him at all times. Whenever he felt down or troubled, he should look at it. The medal was a symbol of hope, of accomplishment, of his future. When Connor was older and won his first medal, he could return that one to his grandfather.

Connor's mother was not enthusiastic about the close

relationship her son had with his grandfather. Janie Allen was not close with her father—never had been. He had been a strict parent. She was a rebellious teenager. She was strong-willed, and so was he, and they often argued. When she was thirteen, her parents divorced. At the age of sixteen, she ran away from home. She married a month later, and it turned out she was four months pregnant with Connor. She and her father didn't talk for nearly two years. When they did, it was only because Janie needed money. Connor's dad was out of work. Bills were piling up. She had no choice but to ask her father for help. He paid off their bills and even helped find Connor's dad a job, a manufacturing job at Bendix. His father had worked there ever since. Then he'd paid the down payment for their first house, just six blocks away from where he lived. His charity didn't buy his daughter's love. Their relationship had deteriorated too much. But, as they drifted farther apart, the relationship his grandfather had built with Connor developed an even stronger bond.

Then, there was the time he saved Connor's life. They had gone fishing like they had done several times before. Connor's grandfather had a cabin with a dock and a small fishing boat on a piece of land nestled in a cozy cove at the Lake of the Ozarks. They sometimes went there on weekends during the summer. It was a peaceful, quiet place. There were few neighbors, and the cove was a great spot for fishing.

They loaded their fishing gear in the boat just before the sun came up that Saturday morning. Fifteen minutes later, they had the boat positioned in a quiet, shaded spot on the other side of the cove, a spot they had been to before. There were fallen limbs and bushes in the water that catfish seemed to swarm to at feeding time. His grandfather stopped the boat about ten feet away and turned off the motor. This was their quiet time. They baited their hooks and arched their fishing lines carefully into an area just in front of the brush and fallen trees. The weights on their lines carried the hooks and bait to the bottom of the lake, where catfish fed. In less than a minute, Connor hooked the first catfish. His fishing rod bowed downward, it was such a large fish, and it was a fighter. The fish first tried to drag the line underneath the brush and tree limbs. If the line got caught or tangled up, it would be easy for the catfish to escape.

Connor stood up in the boat to get a stronger grip on the pole and jerked the fish away from the brush. He lost his balance, fell, and hit his head on the side of the boat as he fell overboard. Connor did not know how to swim. His mother insisted that he wear a life jacket whenever he was in the boat, but he was not wearing a life jacket that morning. When the back of his head hit the side of the boat, he blacked out.

His grandfather jumped in after him. The water was dark and murky and considerably deeper than he thought it would be, considering how close he was to the shore. The old man dove down to the bottom. It was completely dark—he could not see anything. He had to feel with his hands. Two minutes went by without any sign of his grandson. He needed to surface to get more air. When he did, he took one deep breath and dove again, nearly three minutes after Connor had fallen into the water.

Finally, in the murky water, he found Connor's lifeless body. His lungs had taken in lake water. The old man pulled Connor to the boat and lifted him inside, then frantically compressed his grandson's chest while he blew oxygen into his mouth. Nearly five minutes went by. There was no sign of life. With all his force, he pressed down one more time on his grandson's chest. The force caused the boy's body to jump. His mouth opened, and he began coughing up water.

Connor was rushed to the hospital. He would recover without any lasting effects, but that incident would be the last straw for his mother. She would never forgive her father after that day. They would not talk again. Connor was not permitted to go with his grandfather to the lake anymore, but their bond remained strong. He never blamed his grandfather for the incident at the lake. In fact, he owed him his life. So when the time came to say goodbye to his grandfather at the funeral home that day, he didn't hesitate. He took a deep breath, walked to the casket, bent his head down, and said a prayer. Then he reached into his pocket and pulled out the medal his grandfather had given him. That medal had done its job. It was around his neck when his grandfather brought him back to life. It was time for him to start earning his own medals. He bowed his head, thanked his grandfather one last time, slipped the medal back into his pocket and walked away.

His mother had come to the funeral. It was the first time she had seen her father in nearly two years. It was also the first time Connor had ever seen his mother cry. He hoped she had forgiven her father, but Connor never knew for sure. She never talked about him again.

Connor turned down the aisle between the first and second sets of shelving. The body would be a few feet away. But the darkness clouded his vision. He did not see the stranger. As he got closer to where the killing took place, a blanket of fear swept over his body. He began to shake. His legs started to go numb. He began to panic. His chest was pounding. A new nightmare was taking hold when he saw that the stranger's body was gone.

Either he wasn't dead, or somebody moved him. Either way, Connor had to get out of that area quickly. He couldn't see more than a few feet in front of him. He moved quickly toward the back of the basement into the alterations room, watching for someone that might be hiding or might be following him along his path. There were so many hiding places. The stranger could be anyplace. It was so dark. If only he had been able to reach the flashlight that had fallen underneath the shelving, he would be able to see what was in front of him. Without light, he relied on his hearing, so he listened intently as he hurried to the hidden stairway. If the stranger was behind him, he would hear the footsteps. If the stranger was in front of him, hiding, he would hear him when he moved.

Connor got to the door, moving as quickly and quietly as possible. There was a shelf in front of it, obscuring the door from view, which he moved out of the way with barely a sound. Then, before opening the door, he took one last look behind him and listened. He did not see anyone or hear footsteps. Opening the door, he stepped through then shut it most of the way. With the door partially open, he reached with his left hand outside the door to pull the shelf as close to the door as possible. That's when he felt it. A hand, grabbing his hand, trying to pull him out.

CHAPTER 4
THE VOICES ON THE FOURTH FLOOR

Connor struggled to free his left hand. He was slowly being dragged out. The door opened as his body pushed against it. For a second, he looked directly into the stranger's face. He wasn't much older than Connor, but his eyes showed a hardened look that indicated his life experiences had aged him well beyond his years. Blood was caked on his face, neck, and the blue shirt he was wearing—he was the same person that Connor had stabbed with the nail.

The stranger wasn't going to give up. There was only one way this was going to end. Connor lifted the gun with his right hand. He had never shot a gun before—he hated guns, was fearful of them—but that gun was the only thing that could save his life now. Connor pointed the barrel of the gun directly at the stranger, his hand trembling, the gun shaking up and down. The stranger saw the gun, but his expression didn't change. It was probably not the first time someone had pointed a gun at him. If he was afraid, it didn't show. But the fear was certainly showing on Connor's face. He was losing the struggle—his body was most of the way out the door. He desperately tried to hook his right foot against the door frame to give him leverage, but it didn't work. The stranger had the advantage. He had a tight grip on Connor's arm, and in a few seconds, would be on top of him. The gun would be easy to wrestle away. Then the stranger would use it on him.

Connor steadied his hand, closed his eyes, and pulled the trigger. Nothing happened — the safety was on. A smile came across the stranger's face. He knew he had won. He reached for the gun and pulled it out of Connor's hand. Connor closed his eyes. His fight was gone. His life was near an end. He saw his grandfather for just an instant. It must have been a dream. His grandfather said everything would be all right and that it wasn't his time to go. He was there and gone in a fraction of a second.

Then he heard it. The shelf that had been pulled against the door began to topple. It must have been hit during the struggle. The stranger tried to move, but not fast enough. His hand was still holding the gun when the shelving fell on top of him.

The noise was loud. His friends must have heard it, and they would be coming. Connor got to his feet and pulled the gun out of the stranger's lifeless hand. Lifting the shelf off him, Connor knew the stranger was dead. A pair of sewing scissors were protruding out of his neck, apparently having fallen from the shelf when it tumbled over. His eyes were still open. He hadn't had time to close them before his heart stopped.

Connor lifted the shelving up and quickly put the items that had fallen from it back on the shelves. Then he pulled the stranger's body inside the stairwell. He could hear voices, followed by the sound of footsteps. His friends were in the basement now. They would be looking for him. Once his body was completely inside, Connor partially closed the door, pulled the shelving as close to the door as possible, and closed the door. He dragged the stranger's body underneath the stairway. Connor was buying time. The longer it took them to find their friend, the longer it would take them to find Connor.

He wrapped the duffle bag containing the money around his shoulder, picked up the gun, turned, and started up the steps. That's when he saw the flashlight he had dropped the last time he started to go up those steps. He picked it up and turned it on.

The light was weak, but it was still working. There was no way of knowing when its batteries would give out. He would use it sparingly, only when absolutely necessary.

Spider webs dangled from the ceiling near the bottom of the stairs. There were no windows in that stairway, so no light. He could not see more than a couple of feet in front of him. He was terrified. The ghost, the man, whatever he had seen the last time he started up those stairs, might still be up there, waiting for him. But he could not turn back. The strangers were in the basement now.

Connor took a deep breath. Holding the gun in his right hand and the flashlight in his left, he started up the stairs. The old wooden stairs were rotting and made noises when he stepped on them. The weight of his body coming down on them caused them to bend inward. He walked slowly, gingerly, tapping his lead foot down ever so gently on the next step. There was a handrail on both sides of the stairs, but the wood had deteriorated and broken apart in several spots. He needed support in case a stair gave way from his weight. Connor opened the duffle bag, placed the gun and the flashlight on top, and closed the bag. With his hands free, he could use the guard rails for support.

He stopped suddenly. There was a loud noise that sounded like the freight elevator. That's what it had to be. The strangers were in the basement. One or more of them must be using the freight elevator to get to the second or third floor. The elevator would exit in the back room. From there, it was only about sixty feet to the door leading to the hidden stairway. If they found that door, they would be that much closer to finding Connor. He needed to hurry up those steps to get past the third floor. If they got there before he did, Connor would be trapped between them and the basement.

His left foot had stopped hurting — it had gone completely numb. He needed to treat that nail wound. When he was safely on the fourth floor, he would look for something to clean and bandage the wound. He led with his right foot up the stairs and dragged his left foot behind. That forced him to apply more pressure to his right leg and caused him to land with more force on the step. To keep the stair from bowing too much or possibly collapsing, he looked for the path of the nails on each step, where the board was nailed to the underlying support beam. It was the sturdiest part of the step and his best chance of not causing the step to collapse. But in the dark, it wasn't easy to see the row of nails embedded in the step, and he couldn't chance using the flashlight. There were two rows of nails for two support beams, one on each side of the step about six inches from the edge. Once he located the row of nails on the right side of the stair, he stepped up to that stair with his lead foot. Then he would locate the row of nails embedded in the left side of the stair and drag his other foot up to that area. All the time, he held on to the handrail for additional support.

It took him nearly five minutes to get to the second floor, or what he thought was the second floor. There was an old exit sign. The light was out, the glass was shattered, but it clearly pointed to a spot in the wall. But there was no door. It looked like it had been sealed off. He stopped for a minute, listening. He did not hear any voices. If the strangers were in the storage area on the second floor, he hoped he would hear them before they heard him.

Connor proceeded up the stars to the third floor, slowly, carefully. Soon he reached a sign on the wall that notified him that he had reached the third floor. There was another exit sign, but again, no door. It must have also been sealed over, he thought. That's when a wave of panic went through his bones. If the second floor and the third floor were sealed over, then the fourth floor might have been too. If he could not exit, he had no way to escape. He would be forced to wait for the strangers to find him in the stairway or to flee back to the basement and try to hide.

Connor moved up the stairs toward the fourth floor. Three steps from the top, he heard voices talking—a man and a woman, it sounded like. The voices were coming from just above him—from the fourth floor. He continued upward. There was no turning back now.

At the top of the steps was a door. There was no sign indicating that this was the fourth floor, but it must be. There was no exit sign either. He put his hand on the doorknob, and it turned. The door was not locked. He breathed a sigh of relief. There had not been a way to exit on the other two floors. Then, a nervous chill ran down his spine. What about the voices he'd heard? Would someone be waiting for him on the other side of the door?

Connor took out the flashlight from the black duffle bag, lifted it with his right hand, and turned the doorknob with his left. Slowly he pushed the door open and turned the flashlight on. The room was dark. Spider webs covered most of the entrance to the doorway. A gust of cold air pounded Connor as he entered the room. The cold winter air blew through the attic, through the ventilation system, and directly into the fourth floor. Installation designed to keep the cold winter air out had deteriorated over the years. With the heating system turned off to the floor, it must have been twenty degrees colder on that floor than any other part of the building. His body shook as a cold chill ran through him.

He closed the door behind him. Connor was in the backroom on the fourth floor. The light from the flashlight was dim, only illuminating the area a few feet in front of him. A large wooden table was directly in front of him. On it were tools, scissors, a hammer, a screwdriver, a staple gun, and a box of nails and screws. Next to the tools was a lamp. Connor moved to the lamp and turned on the switch, but nothing happened. He looked under the lampshade—the light bulb was missing. Then he thought that light wouldn't have worked anyway. There was no electricity on that floor.

He moved slowly to the right of the table. In front of him was a row of mannequins. He found that funny. It was the mannequins in the basement that provided him a hiding place earlier in the evening. Now he'd discovered their friends on the fourth floor. Would they provide him another hiding place that evening? Then he noticed it. There was something unusual about these mannequins. They were different from the ones in the basement. They had clothes on, each well-dressed — seven male mannequins, seven female. Their clothes looked new — not modern, but new, as if they had come right off the shelf. But not a shelf in today's stores. One male mannequin was wearing a leisure suit. A woman mannequin was wearing a mini skirt. Another wore bell-bottom jeans. The clothes even had a fresh, new smell to them. The clothes those mannequins were wearing were from another time. They were clothes that were in style a decade earlier.

There was something else too. That back room was cold, damp, musty. But the clothes were warm. He shined the flashlight on the face of one of the mannequins. It looked new. There was no dust, no cobwebs, no discoloration. They shined as if they had just been on the showroom. He moved closer to the door leading into the showroom area of the fourth floor and heard a noise. It sounded like laughter. There was light coming from the showroom, beaming out of the bottom of the small openings between the door and the frame and the door and the floor. Suddenly, his flashlight went dark — the battery was dead. He put it back in his duffle bag and pulled out the gun. If someone was behind that door when he opened it, Connor might need to use it. He disengaged the safety and pointed the gun directly in front of him.

***

Ron Caldwell had a colorful past. He grew up in a shack with a dirt floor in a crude mining camp in Jenkins, Kentucky. The shack had no running water and no indoor plumbing. A communal outhouse was used as a bathroom, and communal showers, one for men and one for women, were about fifty yards away. Rows of identical wood shacks made from cheap plywood lined both sides of a dirt road about two hundred yards from the entrance to the mine. A wood stove, one in each shack, doubled as a stove and a heater in the winter. The shacks were all identical, with one bedroom, a kitchen, and a living area all encased in about four-hundred feet of total living space. The shack provided some shelter from the elements but did little to keep out the heat, cold, and rain. The roofs were made out of tin. Rain and wind that hit the roof amplified throughout the shack.

His father had taken the job at the cool mine in 1932. He never meant to stay long. The depression had made it difficult to find work, and the coal mine was hiring. He took a job there, hoping to move on when things got better, but that day never came.

The camp where the coal miners lived was owned by the coal mine. They supplied everything—housing, a grocery store, a medical clinic, and a school. There was even a small church in the camp. There was no need for a miner or his family to go elsewhere. That was a good thing because the nearest town was thirty miles away. Besides, most miners didn't own a car and had no way to travel. Even if they did have the means to travel, they couldn't afford it. The owners of the mine made sure of that. Everything in the camp cost much more than it would elsewhere. Most miners owed the coal mine more than they were earning. Paychecks were rarely paid because earnings were being applied to outstanding debts.

Ron Caldwell spent his childhood in that camp. He went to school there from first to eighth grade. He begged his father to let him continue in school and get his high school diploma, but that wasn't going to happen. The family had debts. They needed the extra income that he could bring in working at the mine. That wasn't uncommon. Most male students were expected to go to work in the coal mine after graduating eighth grade. Most females dropped out of school after the eighth grade too. Many were expected to stay at home, take care of the younger children, cook, and clean until they found a man to marry. Most married by the time they turned fifteen.

Ron Caldwell went to work in the coal mine, as was expected, at the age of fourteen. That lasted three days. He hated the damp, cold darkness within those caves, and he hated the smell of smoke, coal dust, and sweat. The harsh conditions and the back-breaking work were not a life he wanted for himself. Ron had bigger aspirations for his life, so he hopped on a freight car heading west. The young Caldwell didn't particularly care where it took him, as long as it was far away from those coal mines. The young Ron settled in Kansas, moved in with his grandmother on his mother's side, went back to high school to get his diploma, worked at whatever he could find, saved as much as he could, and when he had a good amount saved, he applied for enrollment at the University of Kansas.

He met Rose at KU. He was a senior in the College of Architecture, she was a freshman. They met at a fraternity party, and it was love at first sight for Ron. It took a while for Rose to warm up to him, but persistence paid off, and two days before his graduation, he proposed. She said yes. They were married two months later in a small Lutheran church in Prairie Village, KS. Ron Caldwell went to work at an architectural firm in Kansas City. Rose gave birth to their only child, Connor's mother, ten-months after they were married.

Long hours at work, traveling, drinking, and a series of affairs damaged the marriage, and when their only daughter, Janie, was thirteen, they divorced. Janie never forgave her father. Their relationship deteriorated beyond repair. He rarely saw his daughter after the divorce. Rose did her best to reconcile them, but both were stubborn. When Janie turned sixteen, she ran away from home and got married a few months later. She lied about her age, saying she was eighteen so she wouldn't need her parent's approval. Her mother learned about her marriage two days later. Her father learned about it two months later. Connor was born five months after the wedding.

Ron Caldwell came to see his grandson at the hospital. It was the first time he had seen his daughter in years. They talked, but only briefly. The door to their relationship was opened, ever so slightly, that day. He held his grandson. He shook hands with his son-in-law. He left with the hope that he and his daughter would have a second chance at a relationship, and for a while, they talked and tried to communicate. But when Ron divorced Rose and soon after announced that he was getting remarried, the door to their relationship was shut again. News of his new marriage opened old wounds. Janie, although invited, didn't attend the marriage of Ron and Denise Caldwell. It would be two years before they spoke again.

Ron Caldwell was persistent in trying to have a relationship with his grandson. Through his son-in-law, he was able to keep in contact with Connor. Eventually, Janie warmed to the idea of him visiting with Connor. As trust grew, he was even able to take Connor to his cabin at the lake once in a while. That was until Connor fell out of the boat and nearly drowned. The door to his relationship with his daughter was shut permanently after that.

Ron Caldwell's marriage with a much younger woman was good for a while. Their age difference, coupled with his traveling and long hours at work, eventually caused cracks in their marriage, leading to his wife's affair with David Morgan. It wasn't her first affair. Ron suspected his wife of cheating. He had accumulated considerable wealth over the years, and so before he married Denise, he insisted on her signing a prenuptial agreement. In it, if there was infidelity on her half during the first five years of marriage, she would not be entitled to any compensation in the event of divorce. When he suspected his wife of cheating, he hired a private investigator to follow her. When the investigator returned with evidence of his wife's infidelity, her distraught husband did not react the way he thought he would. He was angry. He wanted revenge.

Ron bought a gun and told her he would be out of town. Then he followed her. When the two lovers entered Adler late that Saturday night, he watched them. David Morgan should have locked the door behind him. He didn't. Ron hid and waited. When the two took the elevator upstairs to the fourth floor, he watched. The sight of his wife in the arms of another man was more than he could take. When the jealousy inside him boiled over and took control, he took the elevator up to the fourth floor. He never intended to kill anyone. He only wanted to scare them. But when he saw them naked and fully engaged in passion, he lost control. David saw him and ran. Ron had never shot a gun before. He was not a good shot. Two bullets missed his wife's lover. He steadied his hand for the third and fourth shots. His target was only inches away. The first wounded his wife. The second shot silenced her screams. It was then he realized what he had done. It was only after his wife was dead that he decided to kill himself. He placed the gun to his temple and fired.

Connor couldn't help but think that perhaps they were the voices he heard coming from the back room. Their bodies were carried away the night of the murder, but their souls remained. Connor hesitated at the door to the showroom on the fourth floor. He was afraid to open that door, but he knew he had to. He steadied his gun, turned the knob, and slowly opened it.

What Connor saw inside the showroom on the fourth floor sent chills down his spine. He froze in place, and his gun dropped to the floor. Conner closed his eyes, waited a few seconds, and re-opened them. Then he shook his head as if he were trying to wake up from a dream. What he saw would not register with his logical thoughts. This couldn't be real, he thought. He was certain he had fallen asleep and was in the middle of a dream, or maybe a nightmare.

CHAPTER 5
ONE DRINK TOO MANY

Thomas Adler married Mary Elizabeth Warren in September of 1932. They had only met three times. It was a marriage born out of necessity. Thomas's father, Aaron, had lost a small fortune during the stock market crash on Black Thursday, October 24, 1929. But he was confident the market would go back up just as it had so many times before. Instead of selling his stock and taking the losses, he bought more stock on margins. Margins were a sort of loan that allowed investors to buy more stock than they had money to pay for. But the market did not bounce back. Instead, Black Thursday was followed by Black Monday, and finally Black Tuesday. When the market finally hit rock bottom, the stock market was down almost eighty-nine percent, and the losses were over thirty billion dollars.

Aaron Adler would have been forced to sell his thriving department store if it wasn't for the Warren family. They owned a large group of funeral homes and cemeteries throughout the Midwest. That turned out to be an even more profitable business with the beginning of the Great Depression. Suicide rates were climbing, people were starving to death, and death from heat and brutal conditions caused by a great drought that hit the Midwest brought additional business to the Warren family. They prospered while the Adler family was trying desperately to hold on. So, behind closed doors, what amounted to an arranged marriage was worked out between Thomas Adler and Mary Elizabeth Warren. The Warren family would buy into Adler department store, providing Mr. Adler enough capital to pay off his margin call. The Warren family ownership in the department store would last five years until the elder Adler turned the business over to his son. At that time, the Warren family ownership was transferred to Thomas and Mary Adler. It was their store to run from that point on.

Despite his father's warning, Thomas invested heavily in the stock market starting in 1932. He happened to buy in at its low point and rode the market all the way up. He made a fortune. He had a knack for picking the right stocks at the right time. Unfortunately, he wasn't as talented at running a department store. He put in neither the time nor effort that the store required. Luckily, he had Mary. She loved the store. She was an astute buyer, a great manager, had an eye for fashion, and a pulse for what well-heeled women wanted in a department store. Thomas was the figurehead—his wife was the one that made the store successful.

Linda Adler grew up in that department store, six days a week. She was strong like her mother. She always knew that someday she would take over the store from her parents—she just didn't think it would be as soon as it was. When she was nineteen, her mother died from pneumonia. Her father was devastated. He lost interest in almost everything except the bottle. If the store was going to survive, Linda Adler would have to make it happen. She was a freshman at KU and had just met a boy named David Morgan. She would leave school to run the department store. David followed her after he graduated that spring. They married shortly after.

There had been more than one murder on the fourth floor of Adler. Long before Ron Caldwell took the life of his wife and then killed himself, there was another murder. That murder didn't make the newspapers either. In fact, only one person knew a murder had even taken place.

David Morgan had weaknesses. He drank too much, he liked to gamble, and he liked women, lots of women. His moral fiber was extremely fragile. He had never earned an honest day's work. But David had a plan. Money would solve all his problems. He needed it. His father-in-law had it. With the death of Mary Adler, Thomas Adler was the only person that stood in the way of his wife inheriting a fortune. And his wife would be the only person standing in the way of him inheriting a fortune.

David had played his wife well. She loved and trusted him. She would do anything he asked of her. So when he asked his wife to set up a meeting between him and her father so he could discuss an investment opportunity, she was happy to do so. She believed in her husband. He was a man with creative ideas. He was always one investment short of making a fortune.

The trouble was that Thomas Adler had lost faith in his son-in-law years earlier. He saw David for what he was, a scoundrel. He was a user of people, a self-centered person that preyed on the trust and love of his daughter. The elder Adler had no use for his son-in-law, but he loved his daughter very much. So when Linda begged her father to meet with her husband to discuss an investment opportunity, he hesitated for a minute and then agreed to meet with him.

The meeting was set up for Saturday night, after the store closed, on the fourth floor. Since his wife had passed away, Thomas spent long hours at the store. He was there before the doors opened and stayed until well after the store closed six days a week. The fourth floor of Adler was where he entertained all his well-heeled customers. It was where he conducted all of his business meetings. The floor was his home away from home, with a fully stocked bar, two large stone fireplaces, comfortable couches, and elegant furniture. It was every bit as nice as the furnishings in his own home. He even had a large office in the back room with a bed and a shower. If he was too tired to make the drive home at night, he would spend the night at the store. With his wife gone, the big mansion in Lenexa was lonely.

He began spending more and more nights in his office. The only time the mansion showed any life anymore was on Sundays. That's when his daughter, son-in-law, and grandson would come over for supper. It had been a tradition in the family when his wife was alive, and Mr. Adler kept the tradition going after her death. It was the only time during the week that he saw his grandson. It was also one of the few times during the week that he saw his daughter. Ever since Dennis was born, David had insisted that his wife stay home. But Adler was in her blood. She would often visit the store, Dennis in hand, to see how her father was doing.

She loved Adler. Her father did not. It was a job to him — it was life to her. She gave her father ideas and advice that aided in the success of Adler. She rarely told her husband about the times she spent in the store. He would not approve and would be upset. His image of an ideal wife was a stay-at-home mom that took care of the kids, cleaned the house, and had dinner waiting on the table when he came home at night. He wanted to control his wife so he could play. David never had a job, yet he was gone all day. He had his demons. They visited him between nine in the morning and seven at night six days a week. Linda never asked her husband what he did with his days. She was afraid he would tell her, and she loved him too much to know. He was attentive to her and Dennis when he did come home. He was gentle and loving. That was all that mattered to her. So she ignored the smell of scotch on his breath and the scent of lady's perfume on his clothing.

Thomas Adler didn't want to meet with his son-in-law that Saturday night. He would have preferred to meet with him the next afternoon when his daughter was present. He didn't like David, didn't trust him. He wouldn't admit it, but he was also afraid of his son-in-law. *Why did he insist on meeting on a Saturday night after the store is closed and not on Sunday after our family dinner?* he thought to himself. His daughter had an explanation. The investment opportunity was confidential. Her husband wouldn't even tell her what it was. He needed to meet in private, with her father's undivided attention.

Thirty minutes after the last employee left Adler that Saturday night, Thomas let his son-in-law in the store. They took the elevator up to the fourth floor. He could smell the heavy aroma of a fine, single malt scotch on his son-in-law's breath. The smell overwhelmed the elevator on the ride upstairs. Thomas wanted to meet in the showroom on the fourth floor—David insisted on meeting in his father-in-law's office. But first, he needed a drink. He stopped at the bar on one side of the showroom floor. He glanced over the bottles of scotch on the shelf behind the bar, picked out an unopened bottle of Glenlivet single malt, and poured himself a tall glass. He insisted that his father-in-law join him in a drink. Mr. Adler protested, but his son-in-law poured him a drink anyway. David was drunk. There was no arguing with a drunk, so Thomas took the drink that his son-in-law handed him. Then David picked up the bottle and his glass, and they proceeded to the office.

Mr. Adler just wanted to hear what David had to say and get rid of him. He had no interest in drinking with him or spending any more time than he absolutely had to with him. But that wasn't David's plan. He downed the first glass of scotch like it was water and poured a second. He insisted that his father-in-law drink with him. Thomas soon discovered that his son-in-law had no interest in talking about an investment opportunity. Even if he had wanted to, he was too drunk to do so. He listened as David talked about his marriage and his son.

"I want more from life. I deserve more," he said.

David told his father-in-law that he no longer loved his wife and that he had stayed in a loveless marriage. His son's behavior issues had added stress to the marriage, and he was upset that his wife had insisted on sending Dennis to boarding school rather than keep him at home. Linda was too controlling. She belittled him, and until now, there had been little he could do because of his dependency on his wife's money, and ultimately his dependency on Thomas Adler. Thomas watched as the darkness rolled into his son-in-law's eyes. He watched the anger change the color of his face to deep red.

For the first time in his life, Thomas Adler was deathly afraid. He looked around for anything to protect himself, for any way to escape. Then he began to feel it. His heart was moving rapidly, and he was struggling to breathe. David pulled out a bottle from his pocket and sat it on the table next to the nearly empty bottle of scotch. Strychnine poisoning mimicked a heart attack. It didn't take much, a few drops in his glass of scotch. David pulled down the covers of the bed. With his father-in-law gasping for his final breath, he moved him to the bed in his office. He removed his clothes and dressed him in his pajamas. He covered him and placed his head face up on a pillow. Then he watched the life drain out of his father-in-law's body.

The next day, Linda and David showed up at Mr. Adler's mansion, like they had every Sunday afternoon for years. They had spent the morning at church and were looking forward to a mid-afternoon supper of fried chicken, mashed potatoes and gravy, and sweet corn. Thomas had become quite a cook over the years. He was a man of many talents.

The house was locked, and there was no sign he was home. He had never missed Sunday supper before. Linda Adler knew something was wrong. She used her spare key to let herself in. Together the couple searched the house. They found nothing. In fact, there was no evidence he had come home the previous night.

"You were with my father last night at the store, weren't you?" she asked her husband.

"Yes, we met in his office on the fourth floor until a little past midnight," he said.

"When you left him, was he okay?"

"Yes, he was excited about the business opportunity I discussed with him. We had several drinks, and I left. He seemed a little tired, but otherwise, he was fine and in good spirits."

Linda and David got in their car and drove to Adler. Linda unlocked the front door, and both walked inside. The lights were still on. That was unusual. Her father always turned out the lights, except for the security lights in the windows and on the perimeter of the building, before he left the store.

"Did my father leave when you did, David?"

"No, he said that he had a little more work to get done before he left, so he walked me to the front door and locked it behind me when I left."

Linda Adler was extremely worried. She rushed to the elevator to take her upstairs. David followed. The creaky old elevator was slow. It seemed to take forever to get to the fourth floor. Linda's heart was racing, her eyes focused straight ahead. Finally, the elevator stopped, the doors opened, and she rushed out. All the lights were still on in the showroom. She screamed out her father's name. There was no response. She hurried to the back room. The lights were on there too. Her father would never leave the lights on if he left the store, and he would not leave all the lights on if he chose to spend the night.

The door to his office, where he would sometimes spend the night, was closed. Light showed from underneath the door frame.

"Linda, maybe I should go in first," David suggested to his wife. That wasn't going to happen. His wife was determined to be the first one through that door. She turned the doorknob and stepped inside. David Morgan waited.

***

What Connor saw on the other side of the storeroom door of the fourth floor that night could not be explained by any measurement of reality he had ever known. The showroom he saw could only exist in some sort of parallel universe or within the darkest crevasses of his mind. He saw in front of him a world where the line between sanity and insanity was blurred. As he looked into the showroom, Connor couldn't help but wonder, on which side of the line was he standing?

In front of him was the fourth floor in all its glory. Elegant chandeliers adorned the ceiling. Fine furniture, polished and looking brand new, encompassed the areas around two large stone fireplaces on opposite ends of the room. Polished cherry wood floors shined and sparkled under the glow of the chandeliers. The walls were covered with fine paintings. A red carpeted walkway led from the wall separating the back room from the showroom. It led to the seating around one of the stone fireplaces. An identical red carpeted walkway on the other side of the room led to the seating area around the other fireplace.

A bartender, dressed in a tuxedo and a top hat, stood behind the bar making drinks. A waitress wearing a full-length dress that flowed down to her ankles, with a strand of white pearls around her neck, waited on the other side of the bar for her order. Logs were burning in both fireplaces, which people were seated near on the furniture. They were talking, they were laughing. The men were gathered together at one of the fireplaces, smoking fine cigars and drinking expensive whiskey. The women were gathered at the other fireplace, drinking wine and eating finger sandwiches. The clothes they were wearing were from a time long ago. The women wore conservative dresses that covered their arms and shoulders and flowed down to their ankles. The men wore black tuxedos and top hats.

There were about a dozen women, not as well dressed as the ones seated by the fireplace, standing about near both groups of people. Standing near the elevator was a man who wasn't quite as well-dressed as the others. He seemed to be watching over them. He scanned the room, and every so often, he motioned for one of the women standing nearby to come to him. He would whisper in her ear, and she would hurry off to do something. The room was busy. The noise was loud. The man standing near the elevator appeared to look directly at Connor. He said something, although Connor didn't hear what it was. The man motioned for Connor to come toward him. He moved slowly toward the man, then heard a noise behind him. Connor turned to look.

Emerging from a black curtain at one end of the wall that divided the back room from the showroom was what looked like a model, wearing an evening dress and walking slowly down the red carpet toward the group of women sitting near one fireplace. The women stopped talking and turned to watch the woman approaching them. A man in a tuxedo with a top hat and wearing white gloves started playing the piano positioned in the opposite corner of the showroom. The woman walked slowly, elegantly to the end of the red carpet only a few feet from her audience. She stood still for a few seconds, turned around, and stood still a little longer. Then she began a slow walk back to the black curtain. One of the women seated raised her hand, and another lady standing nearby with a note pad wrote down some information. As soon as the model disappeared behind the black curtain, another one came out wearing a different dress. Connor watched as several more women came out from behind the black curtain and walked down the red carpet just like the first one had. All wore different types of clothing—some evening wear, some casual wear, some formal wear, and some swimwear. From time-to-time, a woman seated would motion, and another woman standing nearby would write something in her notepad.

Connor thought he knew what was going on, but nothing made any sense. It looked like he was witnessing what his grandmother had explained was the typical sales process that used to take place on the fourth floor many years earlier. The well-heeled customers sat, drank, and talked, nestled near the fireplace, while models walked out displaying the latest in society fashions. The wives sat in one area making their selections while the husbands talked about business, politics, and sports in a separate area. After the wives made their selections, the chosen clothes, worn by the same models, were paraded out the other end of the showroom to the husbands to make the final decisions. In most cases, the husband simply nodded his head to show approval of the purchase. But every so often, a husband would disapprove, and the item would go back. The husband always made the final decision.

Connor watched the activities in amazement. He wasn't afraid — he felt relaxed. It was like a dream — one of those vivid, wonderful, imaginative dreams. He had the feeling that any second, he would wake up and be faced with reality. But if he was dreaming this, he didn't want to wake up, not yet. He felt safe among the strangers he saw on the fourth floor. He felt at peace, and he felt protected amongst them. So, when he glanced back at the man standing near the elevator and saw him still motioning for him to come over, Connor didn't hesitate. He moved quickly toward the man. When he got close, he remembered. He had seen that man before. His picture hung in Linda Adler's office. He looked exactly the way he did in the picture. He was Thomas Adler, Linda's father. The man was staring right at him and began to smile. Connor smiled back. He held out his hand for Connor to shake. Connor held out his hand and then, nothing. Thomas Adler disappeared.

Connor turned around. Everyone was gone. There were no more ladies sitting by the fireplace. There were no more men sitting by the other fireplace. The drinks they had been sipping, the finger sandwiches they had been eating, the cigars the men had been smoking were all gone. There was no more laughter, no more talk, no more songs coming from the piano. The salesclerks, the bartender, the waitresses were all gone. The fires were out in the fireplaces. He watched as the furniture, one by one, disappeared in front of his eyes, along with the chandeliers. The red carpets were gone. All the paintings on the walls were gone, as were the two black curtains where the models had walked out onto the red carpet. The floorboards underneath his feet were warped and starting to rot. Paint was peeling from the walls. Cobwebs appeared from the ceiling. The room was dying in front of him.

He yelled out. No one responded. Finally, the lights that had illuminated the room from the fireplaces and the chandeliers disappeared. The room had become pitch black. The warmth from the fireplaces that had made the room so comfortable just a few minutes earlier was replaced with cold, drafty air that smelled like rotten tomatoes. Connor moved quickly toward the back room. Just as he got to the door, he heard a noise behind him. Before he could turn around, a heavy metal object made contact with the back of his head. He fell to the floor. His eyes saw the figure of a man standing over him just before he passed out.

CHAPTER 6
A TROUBLED BOY

Dennis Morgan was a troubled child, a casualty of a bad marriage between David Morgan and Linda Adler. Even during his early childhood, his parents' arguments and the absence of love began to create wounds in his soul that would never heal. As a young boy, he rarely saw his parents—mostly, he heard them. Late at night, when they thought their son was asleep, he would hear them scream at each other. Dennis laid in his bed and listened to his mother cry. He would hear his father stumble through the house, drunk and upset. He would hear his father hit his mother and often heard her crash into the wall or furniture or tumble to the floor from the vicious beatings. The violence at her husband's hands would be followed by her panicked screams for help.

Dennis would hide under his blanket and wait there quietly in the dark for the fighting to stop. His heart would race as he tried desperately to stop thinking about what was going on just outside his room. He hid underneath the covers pretending to be asleep, hoping for silence and praying for his mother's screams to stop. When quiet finally arrived, and he knew the fighting was over, he relaxed, waiting, hoping the door would open with his mother checking on him. Dennis just wanted one sign of affection, one sign that she cared enough to check on him before she went to bed. It never happened. It was as if his parents didn't realize he existed. He would fall asleep, wiping tears from his eyes. In the morning, the nanny would come into his room, wake him up, and get him dressed, then walk him downstairs. The house would be empty except for his nanny and the housekeeper. His mother would be gone to work. She normally left before the sun came up. His father would be asleep on the couch in the den, normally with a partial glass of scotch on the table next to him. His father was drunk—he was always drunk and would sleep it off on the couch, then wake-up, shower, and start drinking all over again. It was that small fraction of time, after the shower, after he was dressed, and before that day's drinking had numbed his senses, that gave Dennis some glimmer of hope that he was loved. His father would check in on him and smile, then give him a hug, sometimes a kiss, to show he cared. Then he was gone, out the door until early the next morning, if he came home at all.

His wounds of loneliness became more pronounced as he got older. Dennis stopped socializing with everyone. He rarely talked and kept to himself. After school, he went down to the basement, where he would stay for hours. No one knew what he was doing down there, and no one bothered to ask. No one wanted to know. Sometimes a staff member would hear sounds coming from the basement, like the cries of a small animal suffering. That would last for a few minutes and then stop.

David would be the first to discover what his son did during those times in the basement. They would share a bond as a result of that discovery. The evil he witnessed in his son would bring them close. He helped his son hide the secrets in the basement and the darkness in his soul from his wife and the house staff. The basement doors were locked—only David had the key. No one was permitted to go downstairs, and no one on the house staff ever asked about the basement. Nor did they ever confront Mrs. Adler about the sounds they heard coming from the basement. They were being paid very well to keep problems away from their employers.

But few secrets can be kept forever. Linda would discover how disturbed her son had become. To hide his problems, she shipped him off to a boarding school on the east coast. Her husband was upset—she didn't discuss it with him. He loved his son despite never being much of a father to him. The darkness that consumed Dennis Morgan's soul was much more horrifying than his mother realized. It was much the same darkness that had consumed her husband—like father, like son, so to speak. David had a plan for his son. When his wife sent him to boarding school, it disrupted that plan. For a while after his son was gone, David cleaned up his act. He visited his son at boarding school every chance he got, and he reconnected with his son. They talked, they laughed, they shared stories. For a short period of time, David Morgan behaved like the father he was. Dennis, starving for any sign of parental affection, looked forward to his father's visits. He cleaned up his act, too. His grades improved. His attitude improved. His behavior improved.

But the positives of his life were short-lived. Without any explanation, his father stopped coming to see him. There was a reason, but Dennis would not find it out until he was much older. He only heard that his parents had divorced. Linda explained to him when he came home for Christmas break that his father was gone and wouldn't be coming back. Dennis was devasted. His mother offered no explanation for the divorce and no explanation for why his father had not come to see him. That Christmas was miserable. Dennis was alone again, and his mother was always at work. It was Adler's busiest season, after all. The nanny was no longer employed, and the housekeeper worked shorter hours. He was left alone in that house most of the Christmas break. The day he returned to school, his mother didn't even say goodbye to him. As usual, she had left for work early that morning. A cab picked him up and took him to the airport.

His home became the Westminster Academy. With no love or attention from his parents, Dennis sought friendships from like-minded students at his boarding school. Those people weren't hard to find. Most students at Westminster felt abandoned and unloved. They were sent to the private school because they had some behavioral issues or because their parents just didn't want them around. Many of the students were rebellious, lonely, and desperate for friendship. Dennis could have had his pick of friends. When he wanted to be, he was charismatic. He was intelligent and a born leader. But he had a dark side. It was that side of him that would choose his friends. He sought out friends with a few unique characteristics. First, they needed to be easily controlled. They needed to recognize him as the leader — they needed to be soldiers. Second, they needed to be loyal, to follow his directions, no matter the consequences. Third, they needed to be smart. They could not make mistakes that would have consequences for the group. Fourth, they needed to be morally and ethically corrupt. They, too, needed to have a dark side.

Lawrence Engels, Jr. — "Pole," as Dennis would nickname him — came from a wealthy New York family. His father was a real estate developer. Presently, he was interviewing for his fourth wife. Like the past three, she was young, attractive, and wanted to take a short-cut to wealth. Pole wasn't even sure of her name — Cinnamon, Tiffany, Velvet, something like that, he was sure. Pole hadn't seen his mother since she left the house for rehab when he was five. He was sure his father had paid her off to disappear from his life. Since then, he had been raised by a succession of nannies until his father's second wife got tired of seeing him around the house and persuaded her husband to send him off to boarding school. He had been at Westminster for nearly six years. The nickname of Pole was given to him after a rather embarrassing incident on the playground outside of his living hall. A northeaster had recently plummeted the area with two feet of snow. The boys had been cooped up in their dormitory for two days. They needed a break — they needed to go outside. One of the boys brought a football outside, and a game of catch ensued. Lawrence was not the most gifted athlete. In fact, he had never played football before. When it came to his turn to run out for a long pass, he did so, right into a tether pole that was obscured by the snow. The pole left an imprint on his forehead that lasted for three days. The name "Pole" seemed like an appropriate nickname to Dennis.

Michael Scott became the second boy to join the group of friends. His nickname was "Mouse," largely because he looked a little bit like one. He was short, stocky, with a long, wide nose and big, dark eyes with thick eyebrows. His ears were large and protruded outward from his head. His looks alone would have warranted a nickname of "Mouse," but it was his voice that solidified the name. It had a high-pitched, squeaky, tone to it that made people turn and look whenever he talked. He had been teased about that voice all of his life.

Consequently, Mouse talked very little, only when necessary. He had grown up outside of Tulsa, where his father owned several oil wells. His father was a man's man—strong, tough, athletic, and a born leader. He despised weakness. Mouse had a lot of weaknesses. When he was ten, his father sent him to Westminster to toughen him up. Instead, it just drove him and his father farther apart. Mouse had remained close to his mother until recently when cancer claimed her life.

Gregory Hollinsworth, nicknamed "Steam Pipe," was the last member of the gang of four. He grew up on the North Shore of Chicago. Both of his parents were attorneys. His mother was a partner in a prestigious law firm downtown, while his father was a trial lawyer that defended several high-profile clients. His father traveled for weeks at a time. His mother worked long hours, six days a week. When his parents were home, they were very critical of him, especially his father, who was both verbally and physically abusive to his son.

Steam Pipe held everything inside him and never fought back, no matter how painful the abuse was. That just angered his father, more because the elder Hollinsworth despised his son's weakness. His time at home would have been completely miserable if it wasn't for the love and attention of his nanny. Clara was a kind, thoughtful, attractive young woman, just a few years out of college. She took care of him when his parents were not around. Over time she became much like an older sister to Gregory. She remembered his birthdays, special occasions, and school events. His parents rarely did. She woke him up in the morning, took him to school, picked him up afterwards, fed him dinner, helped him with homework, and put him to bed at night. He would go for days without seeing either parent. Steam Pipe was a gentle soul. Someone would need to push him pretty far for him to lose his temper or hurt someone he cared about. When he came home one evening after baseball practice, he found his father trying to force himself on Clara. That's when the gentle soul exploded. He took the bat he had carried into the house from practice and took aim at his father's head. One day later, the nanny was fired. Three days later, Gregory Hollinsworth was sent to Westminster Academy. The name "Steam Pipe" seemed appropriate, Dennis thought, because like a steam pipe that builds up pressure, eventually the pressure gets too powerful and explodes through the pipe.

Together, the gang of four wreaked havoc on Westminster and anyone that got in their way. The friends went from petty crimes like stealing from the commissary, bookstore, and nurses' office, to much larger crimes. They brought drugs onto campus, mostly marijuana, and extorted money, cigarettes, liquor, and anything of value from other students. They threatened anyone that crossed them or dared to turn them in. The gang of four was feared by other students, and their crimes were covered up by the staff.

Westminster was not in the business of expelling students or even contacting parents over minor issues, their survival depending on the parents' tuition payments and support.

Westminster was a small, private school with a student body of less than one hundred. All were year-round students boarding at the school. Tuition was expensive.

What the parents demanded for their money was discretion. Almost all the boys at Westminster had behavioral issues — most had been in trouble before coming there. Their parents were wealthy — they had to be to afford the tuition, room, and board. The parents of those students were pillars of the community holding powerful jobs, members of an elitist social class. Their sons had been disappointments. Most had tarnished the family name. They were sent to Westminster as a last resort. The school consisted of one large, tall brick building nestled in the middle of fifteen well-manicured acres of prime real estate. The building housed the classrooms, teacher's quarters, dining hall, nurse's office, and commissary on the first three floors, and student living quarters on the upper floors. That building was their prison. They bided their time until graduation. Then they would go on to college — most of them anyway.

Dennis had other plans. He had no interest in attending college. His mother had money. She owned Adler. That store would be his someday. She owed it to him. He would be the fourth generation of the Adler family to manage the store — at least that was what he thought. When he graduated from Westminster, he moved back home, telling his mother he wanted to come to work in the family business and was not interested in going to college. She was disappointed. She had been disappointed a lot with her son over the years. Her son appeared to be trying to better his life. He was polite to his mother, no more arguing, fighting, drinking, or taking drugs. At least that was how he appeared to her. His hair was cut short, he was clean-shaven, dressed better, picked up around the house, and helped his mother whenever she needed it. She couldn't help but think it was an act. But there was a small part of her that wanted to believe he had changed, that he had grown up. Dennis was attentive to his mother. They talked, they laughed together. It had been many years since that had occurred.

Near the end of that summer, Linda decided to give her son a job at the store. He would learn the business from the ground floor up, starting in maintenance. Placing her son in the maintenance department was a way for her to test her son's commitment. The job was dirty and required hard work. It would not be an easy job for anyone, let alone someone that had never worked hard a day in his life. If her son was committed to working his way up the ladder, this would be a good initial test for him.

It was during his time in the maintenance department that he first met Bill Collins. Most maintenance jobs were done after the store closed or before it opened in the morning so as not to disturb the customers. Bill worked that late night, early morning shift, the graveyard shift. He would let Dennis into the store and let him out when his work was done. Many times, they would share their lunch break.

Bill Collins was like the father Dennis wished his dad would have been. They talked, and he listened. Bill showed empathy toward his new friend, and if Dennis needed advice, Bill would provide it, devoid of judgment or ridicule. The old man was never condescending like his father had been. Dennis confided in Old Man Collins about his father and mother. He talked about his difficult childhood, about the fighting between his parents, about boarding school. Bill felt a comradeship with the young man. He, too, felt disdain for people like Linda Adler. She had been born with a golden spoon in her mouth. She never had to worry about where her next meal was coming from or how she was going to pay this month's rent. Linda probably made more money in a year than he made his entire life, lived in a mansion, and drove a new, expensive car. Bill had worked hard his entire life and had not been able to save anything. He had always struggled. He had no use for people that had everything handed to them, especially Linda Adler.

The bond between Dennis and Bill grew strong. Old Man Collins respected the fact that Dennis had started work at his mother's store, in arguably the worst possible job to have, maintenance. Granted, working in the maintenance department was not Dennis's choice, but Bill didn't need to know that. He also liked the fact that Dennis wore jeans and a T-shirt to work, not a suit like a manager or a salesclerk would wear. He looked blue-collar. That was the preferred color of collar for Bill Collins. White collar people had always seemed to look down on him. Even when he was on the police force, his superiors wore suits. They were assholes for the most part. If he was investigating a crime or pulled someone over for speeding or drinking, it was always the men wearing suits that gave him the most trouble. Yes, the security guard felt a kindship with Dennis. The young man reminded Bill of himself when he was young, struggling to make ends meet and determined to make it on his own. He admired Dennis for not taking advantage of his namesake. Bill thought he understood Dennis. He was wrong.

Dennis had worked for over a year in the maintenance department at Adler. He showed up on time every day, worked hard, and didn't complain, and he stopped drinking and using drugs. Dennis had been completely sober for almost fifteen months. No matter what his mother asked of him, Dennis did it without complaint. Her son was playing her game—his mother was getting close to retirement. She would step down in a few years, and then the store and the money would be his. He could wait. After all, Dennis had waited Westminster out. Now was his time to reap the benefits of his patience. There was no one else in the family to hand the store over to. Dennis knew Adler would be his someday. But he, too, was wrong.

His mother never discussed closing the store with Dennis. The first he heard about it was during the Christmas tree lighting ceremony the Friday night after Thanksgiving. Her announcement came as a complete shock to Dennis. He was devastated, having never considered that she would close the store. Her son had always assumed he would take over when she was ready to step down. Depression over his mother's decision turned to anger. Even after she made the announcement that Adler would be closing for good, she provided no explanation to Dennis. Nor did she provide any hope for him. She did not plan to support him after the store closed. He would need to move out of the mansion and find a job.

He wanted to kill his mother and considered it for a day or two. If he could do it without fear of getting caught, he probably would have set that plan in motion. Instead, his mind settled on a different course of action. He would steal from her. Not from her exactly, but from her store. Adler was insured. His mother would not suffer a financial loss, not that it really mattered to him. He liked the idea of his mother suffering a little bit.

He talked to Old Man Collins and told him what his mother had done to him and of his plan to get back at her. It was Bill that planned the break-in at Adler. It was him that turned off the door alarm. It was him that opened the door for the gang of four. Bill Collins was to get twenty percent of the take that night. He didn't know that Dennis had a different plan. When Bill opened the back door and saw the four men standing there with no gloves and no face masks, he knew something was wrong. Then Dennis raised a gun to him, and he tried to run. But the young men were faster, and when they hit him and dragged him down to the basement, he knew he would never live to see the money that was promised him. They put a gun to his head in the basement and asked him if anyone else was in the building. He knew if he told them about Connor, his life would end that night also. Bill Collins saved Connor's life that night just before he gave up his own.

The gang of four were Dennis and his three friends from Westminster. He had called them three days after his mother announced that she was closing the store. Each was in college. They would spend Christmas break together in Kansas City. It was a reunion of sorts. They would party, smoke a little weed, rob the store, and spend Christmas in the Adler mansion. It was their idea of fun. Pole, Mouse, and Steam Pipe had no idea that murder was part of the plan.

CHAPTER 7
A COMMON GOAL

Connor's head was pounding. When he opened his eyes, he saw nothing but the dark. He was lying on a bed, on his back. Connor's hands were tied, as were his feet, and blood coated the rope in places where it had dug too deeply into the skin. His left foot was throbbing. Connor's memory of what happened to him was foggy. After stepping back into the back room, the only thing he remembered was the pain of something hitting him over the head. That's when he fell to the floor, and everything went dark. The memory of the people in the showroom was still vivid in his head, but he couldn't be sure if it was real. If it was a dream, he'd felt safe inside it. He wished he could go back to it because wherever he was now was not safe. Whoever had tied him up had a purpose for him that could not be good. Was it one of the strangers that had killed Old Man Collins and were stealing from the store? Then something dawned on him. *Shit*, he thought. Where was the black duffle bag with all the money? Did the person that was holding him captive find it?

Connor tried desperately to loosen the ties to his legs and wrists, but it was no use. They were tight — he could not move. He scanned the room. There was a desk against one wall with a lamp on top of it. It looked like the electrical cord to the lamp ran along the floorboards and fell through a hole drilled in the floor. There was another electrical cord going in the same hole. Connor followed it with his eyes. It led to a small refrigerator tucked next to a closet where men's clothes were hanging. Next to the bed was a small dresser. Someone lived here, he thought. Maybe it was the person that tied him to the bed. There was something else too. It was warm in the room. A vent on the floor next to the desk was blowing warm air into the room.

Connor could hear soft voices. It was difficult to make out the words, but he definitely heard voices, like two men talking with a slight echo. He looked around for the source. It sounded like the voices were coming from the same vent that was blowing warm air into the room. His heart was racing—he could hear it pounding. He tried to relax. Maybe he could make out what they were saying if he could just quiet his heavy breathing.

Then he heard footsteps, loud, heavy footsteps, coming closer and closer to the bedroom door. His heart began to race faster. He listened as the sound of the footsteps stopped just outside the door, then watched as the doorknob began to turn. Connor closed his eyes and laid motionless, pretending to be asleep. The door opened and shut again. Light from the lamp next to him suddenly penetrated his tightly closed eyes. The footsteps moved closer until they stopped just inches from his bed. The sour smell of rotten breath immersed his nostrils, making him struggle not to gag. He could hear the heavy breathing of the stranger next to his bed. Someone breathing inches away from his face. He could smell the perspiration and body odor from someone that hadn't taken a bath in a long while—the smell was nauseating. Connor tried to slow his breathing so as not to take in too much of the odor at one time. Perhaps the stranger would think he was asleep and leave the room.

Then a cold hand fell on his face. It startled Connor, and he jerked and opened his eyes. The man standing next to him was old, seventies, he thought. His eyes were dark, his face and hands worn and weathered. His clothes were dirty, torn, and wrinkled, and he looked as if he had been wearing them for some time. The stranger did not have an angry look, but it wasn't a happy one either. He checked the ties that bound Connor's ankles and hands and looked Connor over for several seconds before he spoke.

"Are you one of the people that broke in tonight?" he asked.

"No," Connor said. "Do you know who they are?"

The old man did not answer. "Are you a good ghost or a bad ghost?"

Connor gave the stranger a curious look as if he didn't understand the question. "I'm not sure what you mean."

"Are you a good ghost or a bad ghost?"

"I'm not a ghost. I work here. I've worked here for nearly two years, every Saturday night."

"I've never seen you before. You've never been to the fourth floor before," the old man said.

"No. I've only been on the other floors."

"Then how did you get here, and who told you about the fourth floor?"

"Bill Collins told me about the fourth floor, and I came up on the hidden staircase in the back of the basement," Connor said.

"Did he send you with my food?"

"No. Bill Collins is dead. The intruders killed him tonight," Connor said.

A frightened look came over the old man. "Bill is my friend. He has been taking care of me. If he is dead, then they know where I am. They will be coming for me soon. They'll want to kill me." The old man's hand grabbed Connor's neck and tightened his grip. "I need to know, right now, are you a good ghost or a bad ghost?"

"I'm neither. I told you, I work downstairs. Bill told me about the fourth floor. He told me how to get up here. I was trying to hide from the intruders. One of them, the leader, I think, shot him, and I thought I would be next if I didn't hide. When I thought it was safe to escape the basement, I headed to the stairway. But one of the strangers found me. I thought he was going to kill me. I pointed a gun at him, but he took it away from me. He was just about to shoot me when a large shelf fell on him, and he dropped the gun. He was dead. I dragged him underneath the staircase, hoping they wouldn't find him, and then I started upstairs."

"Where did you get the bag with all the money, and how'd you get the gun inside the bag?" the old man asked.

"You found my bag? Where is it?"

"I've hid it. Where'd you get the money and the gun?"

"Loosen my arms and legs a little bit, and I'll tell you. They're too tight."

The old man loosened the ropes binding his hands and feet. Then he stared at Connor with a stern look. "Where did you get the money and the gun?"

"When I was trying to escape to the hidden staircase, I stepped on a nail and made a noise. The stranger heard me and came looking for me. When he found me, I fought him to get away. In the process, I stabbed him with the nail. I thought I had killed him. I grabbed his gun and started to run toward the stairway, but then I remembered Bill Collins. I thought he might still be alive. So I went back to the security office to check on him. I found him in the closet covered in blood. I don't think he is alive. When I left the room, I saw the black duffle bag lying on the floor in the accounting room. It was filled with money, the money from the safe. I took it, thinking that I could use it to bargain for my life if I needed to. On my way back to the staircase, I went to check on the stranger I thought was dead. He was gone. I must not have injured him too badly. He caught up to me at the staircase."

The old man began to smile. "That explains a lot," he said. "Let me ask you something. Just before that shelf fell over and killed the stranger, did you hear someone? Or did you feel something? Like someone else was there?"

"Yes, I thought I heard my grandfather assure me that everything would be okay. But that's impossible. He died when I was young."

"That's one of the good ghosts," the old man said. "If you've got the good ghosts on our side, you might have a chance to survive the night."

"What are you talking about? I don't believe in ghosts," Connor said.

"You still don't believe in ghosts even after what you saw in the showroom earlier tonight?"

"That wasn't real. It had to be a dream," Connor said.

The old man laughed. "Listen, kid. I know I look crazy. Hell, I may be crazy. But one thing that I am absolutely sure of is that those ghosts are real. They come out every night. At least, I hear them every night. For a long while, I thought they were in my head too. I thought I was going crazy. You see them, you hear them, but they never talk to you. It's the same people every night. They're ghosts from a time long ago, a time when the showroom on the fourth floor of Adler was a place that only the best of Kansas City society went. They have relived the same night every night for years. No one knows that they exist except me, and now you, and the bad ghosts, of course."

"Who are the bad ghosts?" Connor asked.

"They live in the walls of the fourth floor. They come out at night after the good ghosts have gone to sleep. I hear them through the vents. They don't like the good ghosts. They won't enter the showroom because that is where the good ghosts live. They only haunt the hidden room beyond the vents. The hidden room is not safe. They will hurt anyone that goes into their room— the good ghosts like you. You can talk to them. Maybe they'll let me hide in the showroom. That's the only place I'll be safe. They won't let me in their room. But maybe you can convince them to let me hide there. If you promise to ask them, I will untie you. Will you ask them?"

Connor was convinced the old man was insane. He must have lost his mind. He looked like he hadn't changed clothes or bathed in months. What was he doing hiding on the fourth floor? Obviously, he had been living there for some time. Where was he getting food? Where was he getting drinks? Why did he bandage Connor's foot but tie him up afterward? Why did he hit him over the head in the first place? Connor was fearful of him. He was crazy. He was unpredictable. But he might be Connor's only chance for survival if those intruders decided to come up to the fourth floor. He decided to appease his captor. He needed to earn his trust so he could get out of the binds that tied him to the bed.

"I'll talk to the ghosts for you," Connor said.

Like he promised, the old man untied Connor. He went to the refrigerator and pulled out a bottle of water. He handed it to Connor.

"Thank you," Connor said with a smile on his face. He held out his hand for the old man to shake it. "My name is Connor. What is yours?"

"My name is David Morgan," he said.

Connor knew that name. It was the name of Linda Adler's ex-husband.

"Can I ask something, David?"

"Depends on what you want to ask."

"How did you come about living on the fourth floor?"

"That was Bill Collin's idea. He was my friend. I knew him when I was still married to Linda. He didn't like her much. She can be a challenging woman. Bill was on the Kansas City police force when the murder-suicide on the fourth floor took place. He helped cover it up and keep it out of the newspapers. My ex-wife paid him well for doing it. After Linda divorced me, I went through a difficult time. I drank too much, gambled too much, and experimented with drugs. I lost everything I had, including contact with my son. Bill found him and brought him to me. He used to hate me, but not anymore. Now he only hates his mother.

That's why this robbery tonight was planned. Dennis was going to rob Adler with the help of Bill Collins. The money was going to be split, half going to Bill and half going to Dennis. Bill was going to split his half with me. He was the only friend I had left. I was homeless, sleeping on the streets when he found me and brought me here. He's been taking care of me ever since. A while back, he even brought my son, Dennis, up here to meet me. If it wasn't for Bill, we may have never reunited. It was Bill's plan to rob Adler, to provide for me and my son so we could take care of each other even after the store closed. You see, Linda had no plans to take care of Dennis or me with the proceeds from the closing of the store. Bill was looking out for both of us.

"But something must have gone wrong. Bill was not supposed to die. You said there were four intruders that came into Adler tonight. The plan only called for Dennis and Bill to rob the store. There wasn't supposed to be anyone else. I can't believe my son would have killed Bill. Someone else must have done it. If that's the case, then Dennis is in danger too. Maybe someone found out about the plan and has taken Dennis hostage to complete the robbery. If that's true, they will surely kill him too when they've accomplished their plan. They probably know I am up here. They may also know that you are on the floor. If they killed Bill, they are not going to leave any witnesses. They will be coming to find us soon. We will need to fight back. We will need the good ghosts on our side. They can protect us."

Connor was certain the old man was crazy. But what if he wasn't? If his story was even close to being true, Bill was not the person Connor had thought he was. He had a dark side that Connor had never seen. Why did Bill bring David Morgan to the fourth floor of Adler, and why had he been taking care of him for so long? Connor didn't believe it was out of friendship. There had to be another reason. Connor was certain about several things. Bill Collins did not know that he was going to die tonight, and he had protected Connor by telling his killers that no one else was in the store. Dennis Morgan was the person that had killed Bill Collins. Dennis knew that his father was on the fourth floor. He had visited him several times, so he knew about the hidden staircase. Connor was also certain of one other thing. The intruders would be coming up that staircase soon. They were not going to leave any witnesses. The old man and Connor would need to fight back for their survival.

Connor was less certain about something else. He had never believed in ghosts before, but he couldn't dismiss what he had seen in the showroom of the fourth floor earlier that evening. What he had dismissed as a dream seemed more plausible when someone else had seen them too. David referred to them as good ghosts. That certainly fit with Connor's encounter with them. He felt at ease, not threatened by them. They seemed happy. They seemed like regular people. Yet, according to David, they wouldn't allow him to enter the showroom. What did they have against him? Why did they allow Connor to enter but not David Morgan? He had spent his entire time on the fourth floor in that back storage room, never going into the showroom. And if the old man was right about the good ghosts, was it possible that he was right about the bad ghosts?

Connor moved slowly toward the showroom door. Unlike the last time he approached the door, there was no light coming through the openings at the bottom and sides. There was no noise either — no laughter, no talking, no indication of life beyond that door. David followed a few steps behind. He had tried opening that door several times before, every time with the same result. He would turn the handle to the door and could hear people on the other side of it, laughing, talking, drinking. It sounded like a party. The door would open a few inches, and then it would slam shut. When he tried to turn the handle a second time, the door would be locked. For the brief second that the door partially opened, David Morgan felt at peace. He felt safe. He felt like everything on the other side of that door was good. It reminded him of a simpler, more peaceful time in his life. It made him feel so good that he dreamed of being on that side of the door. He'd tried many times to enter, but the good ghosts never let him in.

Connor got to the door and turned the knob. It was totally dark inside. What he could see, a few feet in front of him was bare. It looked like everything had been removed. The floors were bare. The ceiling was crumbling. The paint was peeling off the walls. He began to wonder if he had dreamed everything he saw before.

He stepped into the room three or four feet. When David Morgan began to pass through the doorway, a large gust of wind blew past Connor and directly into David Morgan, pushing him back and knocking him to the floor. The door slammed shut. Connor was alone, in the dark.

Suddenly, the air turned cool. A light could be seen in the flue of both fireplaces. A fog began to come through one fireplace, then the other. The fog thickened and slowly rolled throughout the entire showroom. The fog was blinding—Connor could not see anything.

Then, as fast as the fog appeared, it disappeared. The ghosts were back. The room was alive again with people talking, drinking, laughing, dressed in clothes from a time long ago. The room looked exactly the way it had the first time Connor saw the ghosts. The furniture was antique. Crystal chandeliers dropped from the ceiling. Even the people looked the same. He recognized Thomas Adler again, having seen his picture in Linda Adler's office numerous times. He looked exactly as he did in the picture. He had also seen Thomas Adler the last time he was in this room. And, just like the last time, he was standing by the elevator. He remembered his grandmother's stories about the good old days of Adler when the owner met their best clients at the elevator as they got off on the fourth floor. That elevator had been closed for many years, yet there it was across the room. Connor watched as the elevator moved from the first floor to the second, then to the third, and finally to the fourth floor. The door opened. Thomas Adler stood waiting, and an older man stepped off the elevator.

Connor couldn't believe his eyes. He closed them, then reopened them. Stepping off the elevator and shaking hands with Thomas Adler was Connor's grandfather.

CHAPTER 8
ALL SPIRITS AREN'T GOOD

This wasn't the first time that intruders broke into Adler with the intention of robbing the store. Nearly three years ago to the day, three days before Christmas, a daring robbery attempt took place. Bill Collins foiled the robbery, but the timing of it and the lapse in security that allowed the break-in caused Linda Adler to be suspicious of the only security guard on duty at the time of the robbery, Bill Collins. The robbery attempt happened three hours after an armored car delivered nearly two-hundred-thousand-dollars of precious jewels, including a five-carat diamond ring and diamond necklace that had been purchased by one of Adler's wealthiest customers, Stanley Hunt II, as a Christmas gift for his new bride. Mr. Hunt had planned to pick up his gifts the next morning. Only a few people in the store knew about the jewels and their delivery. Bill Collins was one of them.

About two in the morning, two men dressed in black, wearing ski masks and gloves, lifted a ladder to a fire escape on the west side of the Adler building and climbed to the roof. They walked to an emergency exit door leading from the fourth floor to the roof. That exit had not been used since the fourth floor was shut down. The door had always been locked from the inside. It wasn't locked that night. The strangers climbed down the handful of steps leading to the fourth floor. Years ago, the stairs would have led to a door that would open to the storage room.

But, after the floor was closed, Linda had the door removed, and a wall was put in its place, permanently sealing off the route to the roof of the building. The men got to that wall, turned to a side wall, and used a sledgehammer to knock a hole in it. They crawled inside that space and followed the wall to a large vent. After removing the cover to the vent, they crawled inside a few feet to where it exited into the office at the rear of the storage room. From there, they went down the hidden stairway to the basement. The burglars made their way to the accounting office. In the back of the office was the safe, and inside the safe were the jewels. They drilled a hole through the lock in the safe and opened it. Then, they took the jewels and started back the same way they had come. Everything was going as they planned.

According to Bill's account of that night, he was making his rounds on the first three floors at the time of the break-in. When the safe was penetrated, it set off a silent alarm. The police were notified, but so was Bill. It took the police department twelve minutes to reach Adler. It took Bill Collins eight minutes to reach the robbers. He found them on the fourth floor, just about to enter the empty space behind the wall, and shot them dead. They were less than fifteen feet from escaping onto the roof. The jewels were never recovered. Neither man had them in their possession when the police found them. Bill Collins swore that he saw a third person escape onto the roof. The police never located that person, and the jewels were never found. The security guard was a suspect for a short period of time, but no one could tie him to the crime. He was hailed a hero for stopping the robbers. The insurance company paid the claim on the jewels, and things returned to normal after a few months.

Bill Collins had a dark side. Even during his years on the Kansas City police force, he had a reputation for helping out anyone willing to pay. He had no problem taking a bribe and selling his services to anyone with enough cash. To say he was corrupt would be an understatement. In the '60s and early '70s, the mob took a foothold in Kansas City. They operated out of the Italian section of town just southwest of downtown. That was part of Bill's beat. In the early '60s, the DiGiovanni family and the Civelli family controlled most of the gambling and drugs in the Kansas City market. The DiGiovanni family had control of the northern section of town. The Civelli family had control of the southern section of town. Bill Collins took money from both families. He provided them protection and information.

Both families co-existed peacefully for several years, but it was a peace that was doomed to fail. A large section of Kansas City, south of downtown to the plaza area, was a prime area for selling drugs and prostitution, two of the most profitable enterprises for both families. The Civelli family claimed that territory. The DiGiovanni family wanted it. During the years that the Civelli family claimed that territory, they prospered. They became wealthy. They were able to buy more politicians, more police, and more judges. The DiGiovanni family struggled. They saw their power and influence diminish. The Civelli family was becoming too powerful. The very survival of the DiGiovanni family depended on taking that prime territory.

A war between the two families broke out. The DiGiovanni family struck first, firebombing a restaurant run by the rival family. No one was killed in the first bombing. It was meant as a warning, as an invitation to meet and discuss realigning territory boundaries. The Civelli family wasn't interested in changing the boundaries. They struck back by gunning down several mid-level soldiers of the DiGiovanni family inside a bar that was owned by them. The mob war escalated from there.

Bill Collins could no longer straddle the fence between both families. He had to pick a side. He chose the Civelli family. That decision nearly cost him his life. His home was bombed. In an explosion that rocked the entire neighborhood, he and his wife barely escaped out a rear door just as the house went up in flames. That explosion nearly cost Bill his job. It became obvious that he was targeted because of his affiliation with the Civelli crime family. People in Kansas City were fed up with the violence. The police chief demanded that Bill Collins resign. He refused. He asked for the help of the police union to keep his job. They negotiated a six-month leave of absence with pay. Bill Collins knew too much. He knew who was being paid off by the mob. His information would have crumbled the police department and embarrassed city hall. The police chief felt the six-month leave of absence was his best option.

He and his wife left Kansas City for a short time and went into hiding. The DiGiovanni family put out a hit order on him, but Bill Collins had always been a lucky person. His luck did not fail him this time, either. Two weeks after the bombing of Bill's house, the crime bosses for the DiGiovanni family were arrested in a series of early morning raids. The mob war in Kansas City came to an end. The DiGiovanni family fell apart and ceased their Kansas City operations. The Civelli family took control of all of Kansas City. Bill Collins and his wife were safe. He had picked the right side of the fence.

A few weeks later, he moved back to Kansas City, rebuilt his home, and went back to work. But the Civelli family would not let him go. They owned the dirty cop, and they would always own him. No one walked away from the mob unless it was in a body bag. Bill continued to turn his back on their illegal activities and continued to feed them valuable information. The money they paid him was good. The price that it cost him would never be worth it. He had dug a hole for himself that he could not get out of.

When his wife was diagnosed with cancer, the Civelli family paid the hospital, medical, and cancer treatment costs that insurance would not cover. Bill Collins dug an even bigger hole for himself. Nothing was given for free by the mob. He would eventually pay the cost with interest, but he didn't worry about that while his wife was battling cancer. He loved her—he had always loved her—and he was willing to sign a pact with the devil if it bought him a little more time with his wife. Eventually, the cancer took over her body, and she passed. The mob paid her funeral and cemetery costs. They purchased a grave and large granite monument for her overlooking a pond in the cemetery. His wife died, never knowing that her husband was taking money from the mob.

After his wife's death, Bill Collins wanted to leave Kansas City to start a new life. He wanted out of the control of the mob, and he wanted to retire. But the only way he could retire was with the blessing of the Civelli family. He begged them to let him go—they refused. He owed them too much money. Antonio and Anthony Civelli, the two brothers that were the heads of the family at that time, did come up with one option. The mob's criminal activities had been curtailed recently with the election of a new, tough-minded police commissioner, who had won the job by promising to crack down on drugs and prostitution. The Civelli family needed a new, cleaner income source to make up for what they were losing with the crackdown.

Giovanni Civelli gave Bill Collins three options. One, he could continue to work on the police force and assist the mob. Two, he could end his life. Three, he could take a job that the mob wanted him to take and do exactly what the mob wanted him to do. He chose the third option. Soon after, a series of events happened that opened the door for him to accept a job at Adler. First, the security guard that worked the graveyard shift at Adler was paid a visit by a couple of employees of the Civelli family. As a result of the visit, he decided to retire. Second, Bill Collins was recommended for the Adler security position by some rather persuasive people. She resisted at first. Linda Adler ran an ad in the Kansas City Star in an effort to get a replacement, and Bill answered the ad—so did several other candidates. Bill Collins was not Linda Adler's first or even second choice. She offered the job to two other individuals. Both, after visits from employees of the Civelli family, chose not to accept the job. Bill Collins was the third choice, and he accepted. Linda Adler never fully trusted him. Her gut told her that his motives for taking the job were not genuine. Her gut was right.

Three months into his employment at Adler, he received his first assignment from the Civelli family. A man would arrive at the shipping door at exactly three the next morning. Bill was to turn the alarm and surveillance camera off at two fifty-five and open the door for him when he arrived. The man entered and told him to take him to the accounting office. The security guard did as he was told. The man went directly to the safe, placed a sensitive listening device on the lock and turned the knob until it clicked on the first combination number. He wrote the number down. Then, he turned the knob to the right until it clicked again. He repeated the process to retrieve the third number and finally turned the handle and opened the safe. The whole process only took a few minutes. Afterward, he shut the safe door without removing anything, handed Bill the paper with the three numbers written down, and told him to memorize the numbers then destroy the paper. With that, he left the same way he came in.

A week later, he heard a knock on his door fifteen minutes before he would leave for his night shift at Adler. The stranger at his door was an employee of the Civelli family. He gave Bill his assignment. He was to open the safe during his shift, when no one else was around, remove all of the credit card charges from the safe, take them into Linda Adler's office, and copy them on her copy machine. There was one problem. Linda always locked her office door, the one door Bill did not have a key to. The Civelli family had taken care of that problem. The employee handed Bill a key to Linda Adler's office door.

So every night the security guard worked, he would open the safe, remove the credit card receipts, copy them, and then put them back in the safe and lock the door. He could fit six credit card receipts on one piece of copy paper. Sometimes he would have as many as twenty sheets of paper to sneak out of Adler when he left — he used his lunch bucket to do so. He would always break into the safe after his lunch break when most of his food and all the coffee in his thermos were gone. When he packed his lunch before he left for work, he placed his sandwich and chips in a large plastic bag in his lunch pail. After eating his lunch and drinking his coffee, he copied the credit card receipts, put the copies inside the plastic bag, sealed it, dropped it inside his empty thermos, and walked out of the store the next morning carrying the receipts inside his lunch pail. He was careful to hide the evidence in case someone checked his lunch pail. Nobody did.

Adler was blessed with wealthy clientele. Copies of their credit card receipts were sold on the black market. Purchases made from the stolen credit card information were relatively small and went unnoticed by most of Adler's well-heeled customers. The ones who noticed the illegal charges simply alerted the credit card company, and the card number was changed. No one was able to tie the stolen credit card numbers to Adler. The mob made a considerable profit from Bill Collin's work, but he never saw a penny of it. All money went to pay his debt, with interest. The funny thing about the debt was that it never got paid off.

When banks started cracking down on credit card theft, the Civelli family came up with new and more profitable ways for Bill Collins to pay them back. He spent evenings scavenging through sales receipts and customer files in Linda Adler's office. He looked for addresses, social security numbers, family information, and any embarrassing information that might be used for blackmailing wealthy clients. The sales associates and personal shoppers were trained to document every bit of information about their best clients. Linda Adler insisted that that information was the property of Adler and should remain in the store, in her office, whenever the personal shopper or sales associate was not at work. Bill Collins copied everything he could and turned it over to his contact with the mob. They used the information to get loans in the name of the client, steal money from bank accounts, falsify identities and, on occasion, blackmail someone that has made poor choices. They uncovered affairs, hidden assets, illicit activities, and lies for which some people were willing to pay to keep their secrets from being divulged. There were even notes about vacation information that sometimes was used to rob the home at exactly the right time.

Bill Collins was at the mercy of the mob. Whatever they wanted, he did. The robbery of Mr. Hunt's jewels was ordered by the Civelli family. Bill told them about the delivery. They provided him two of their employees to commit the heist, but it wasn't going to be just a simple robbery. The two employees picked to rob Adler had fallen out of favor with the family — they had stolen from them. Bill was ordered to kill them while they were attempting to escape, then take the jewels and give them to Anthony Civelli. The silent alarm was part of the plan. Bill set it off. He knew once he did that he would have about fifteen minutes before the police arrived. It was just enough time to follow the criminals up the back staircase, shoot them, hide the jewels in a hidden crawl space between the third and fourth floors, and return downstairs to meet the arriving police officers. He made up the story about seeing three intruders and watching one escape after shooting the other two. He thought that story would deflect attention from him when the police were unable to find the missing jewels. It did, but not right away.

The security guard remained a suspect in the robbery for several weeks. He was watched. He was followed. His phone was tapped. He left the jewels in the crawl space for almost two months before he felt safe enough to take them out of the store. The problem was that Linda had recently installed a security system at every exit from the store in an effort to lower the quantity of thefts. The store had experienced an uptick in shoplifting for some time. The theft of the jewels pushed her over the top. The security system she installed was state of the art. Every bit of merchandise in the store was tagged with a magnetic strip that set off the alarm whenever the item went through the security area. As an added precaution, in case the magnetic strip was removed, the alarm would sound whenever diamond jewelry went through the security area. To keep the alarm from going off, a customer that purchased diamond jewelry needed to be escorted to the exit door by an Adler employee, and they would exit through the entrance door, avoiding the security area.

To avoid the security area, Bill Collins would need to take the jewelry out through the roof. A trusted employee of the Civelli family would meet him on the roof and take the jewelry. It had been arranged that that employee would be waiting for him on the roof that night.

It was the time that he came to retrieve the jewels from the crawl space that he first saw the ghosts. He had just retrieved the jewels and put them in his thermos, inside his lunch box, when he heard the sound coming from inside the wall on the fourth floor. It sounded like two people talking to each other. After waiting for a minute, the voices stopped. When he had not heard any sounds for several minutes, he proceeded to the back office where the vent was that would lead to the hidden area and the staircase leading to the roof. He lifted his flashlight, turned it on, and walked to the vent. That's when he heard the voices a second time. It sounded like the voices were coming from the vent. He pointed the flashlight inside — the noise stopped. After waiting a couple of minutes and not hearing the voices, he pulled a screwdriver out of his pocket and loosened the four screws holding the vent screen in place, then lifted the screen and began to climb inside.

The air was cold and damp. Quickly, he moved through the vent. The person the Civelli family had sent was waiting on the roof for him. The voices were quiet. He moved about three feet inside the vent and was at the edge of the hidden room, the

same room that the robbers used when entering the building
from the roof, and the same way he needed to exit the building to
the roof. The area was completely dark and quiet. Bill lifted the
flashlight and turned it on, but there was no light. He tapped it
against the side of the vent, making a loud noise. Then he flipped
the light switch on again. It turned on this time, and he lifted the
light to point directly in front of him. That's when he saw the two
ghosts, men he thought, moving toward him. The sight of them
startled him, and he dropped his lunch box and thermos inside
the vent and moved backwards quickly. They caught his left foot
and pulled him back into the hidden room. In an instant, they
threw him on the floor, on his back. His eyes were staring into
the face of darkness. The looks he saw on their faces would haunt
him for the rest of his days. They were covered in blood, their
faces had decayed, and their bodies were covered in roaches and
spiders. Their eyes were missing. The dark holes that replaced
their eyes followed his every move. He recognized them. The
ghostly figures were the two mob associates he had murdered.

Bill Collins turned his head and ran. The creatures followed
him into the vent. He felt their cold hands grabbing at his legs and
felt their fingers digging into his skin. He knew that if they were
able to grab hold of him, they would kill him. In desperation, he
kicked his feet as he moved his legs through the vent. When he
got out, he ran. Bill didn't slow down until he was halfway down
the rear staircase. When he finally slowed, he turned around to
see if they were still following him. They weren't. He ran the rest
of the way down the stairs to the basement, shutting and locking
the basement door behind him. The ghosts did not follow. When
Bill Collins got back to the security office, he took off his shirt to
assess his wounds—claw marks on his back, legs, and left arm.
He had defensive wounds on his hands that appeared to be knife
wounds. There was no doubt that whatever he encountered in
that room wanted to kill him and would have if he hadn't fought
them off.

But dropping that thermos in the vent on the fourth floor created an even bigger problem for Bill. The jewels would not be delivered to the Civelli family. The mob would not be forgiving. He called Anthony Civelli to tell him that someone inside the building had intercepted him, that he was injured in the struggle, and had dropped the jewels in a vent but could not recover them due to his injuries. Mr. Civelli was not happy and demanded to know the location of the jewels. Bill gave them that information. Their employee waiting on the roof was instructed to break down the door and retrieve the jewels. The man found the thermos exactly where Bill said it would be, grabbed it, and started back to the roof. The ghosts were waiting. He dropped the thermos, then got four shots off. Bill heard the gunfire from his basement office. Then, he heard the screams from the employee that had tried to retrieve the jewels. The employee of the Civelli family would escape to the roof and would manage to get down the fire escape. He would not manage to live long enough to exit the alley behind Adler. Other employees of the Civelli family would come to remove his body from the alley.

Bill Collins did not tell anyone about what he saw that night. He did not go back to the fourth floor, leaving the vent screen open, the hidden crawl space exposed, and the jewels inside his thermos lying inside the hidden room. The Civelli family gave him two days to retrieve the jewels and deliver them.

He had two options, and neither were good. He could go to the fourth floor, retrieve the jewels, and try to escape before the ghosts got to him. Or, he could try to hide from the mob. Neither option appealed to him. Then, he came up with a third solution. He could get someone else to retrieve the jewels for him.

When he found David Morgan living on the streets two blocks from a bar the security guard frequented, he couldn't believe his luck. David knew Bill. He had helped cover up the murder-suicide of David Morgan's girlfriend and her husband. It was easy for Bill to befriend David Morgan. Bill convinced him that he wanted to help and brought David to Adler late that night, took him up the hidden stairway to the fourth floor, and promised to make a place for him to stay there. He promised to provide him food and drink and take care of him. All he asked in return was for David to do him one favor while he waited at the top of the stairway, gave David a flashlight, and instructed him on what to do.

***

It was a small favor, and David Morgan did exactly as he was asked. The vent was narrow, not much larger than his body. The tight space made him feel claustrophobic, but the light from the flashlight that his new friend handed him provided a sight of a larger room on the other side of that vent. It wasn't far, and he crawled as quickly as he could to reach that area before his fear took complete hold of him. When he reached the room, David breathed a sigh of relief and then stood up. The hidden room was about as narrow as a hallway, but the ceiling was tall. The room stretched about twenty feet, and at the end, David could see a stairway leading to the roof. The room, much like an uninsulated attic, provided little shelter from the cold winter night. The lunch box and thermos were lying on the floor in that room, just where Bill told him they would be. He picked them up and proceeded to the hidden staircase and up to the door leading to the roof.

The door was partly open, and cold air from the outside was rushing in. David sat the thermos on the roof directly in front of the door. Then, he started back inside. After making it down the stairs and into the hidden room without incident, he heard the voices of two angry men talking to him. They told him that he wasn't welcome in their space. Then, he felt a cold gust of wind blowing in from behind him and turned to see the decomposing shells of two men. That sight caused him to let out a scream. His instincts were to run, and the only way he could exit that room was through the vent. He rushed to it, fell to the floor, and began crawling as fast as he could. One of the creatures grabbed his foot.

He could feel him trying to pull him back as David kicked and fought to get free. After a few seconds, he slipped away from the creature's grasp and jumped out of the vent on the other side of the wall. They did not follow him. *The creatures were upset because I entered their space,* he thought. David Morgan believed he was safe as long as he didn't open that vent and go inside the hidden room again. But he was wrong.

CHAPTER 9
THE MIND IS A TERRIBLE THING TO LOSE

David Morgan had been riding a tight rope between sanity and insanity for years. Drugs, alcohol, and his time on the streets as a homeless person drove him closer to crossing over to the crazy side of life. That first night on the fourth floor had shut the door on his days of sanity.

He never told Bill Collins about the ghosts. When asked how his trip to the roof went, David only said that it went fine. Bill called the Civelli family, and they came to pick up the thermos containing the jewels. He had cheated death one more time, but he knew the Civelli family would never let him go. His debt to them would never be paid off. Soon they would have more work for him to do.

Bill was true to his word that he gave David. The security guard provided for his new friend just as he had promised. The fourth floor storeroom became David's prison. All the basic comforts of food, clothing, and shelter were provided to him with only one condition—that he never leave the fourth floor. Considering his past time living on the streets, the fourth floor seemed like a good place to call home. Once a night during Bill's graveyard shift, he would visit his friend, and they would talk. Everything the security guard did was calculated. He befriended David because he needed him. He checked on him nightly to gauge his increasing level of insanity. The voices in the wall soon consumed his mind, and Bill needed a reasonably sane David to assist him in carrying out his final plan. David became completely dependent on him.

Bill went weeks without hearing or seeing the ghosts, but David heard them every night. He listened to them through the vent in his room. But their conversations were inaudible. Dave could discern the tone of the conversations — they always seemed angry — but was unable to determine what they were saying to each other. It was as if they were talking in another dimension. The conversations went on all night long, except when Bill was in the room. The ghosts only talked when David was alone. The voices were driving him farther and farther into insanity, like a buzzing noise he couldn't get out of his head. The voices prevented him from sleeping. They prevented him from thinking, from concentrating.

He began talking to the voices in the vent, but they didn't acknowledge him. His reality began to be clouded, and he had difficulty discerning what was real and what was unreal. The visits from his friend provided him his only reprieve from the voices that had taken over his mind. That was the only time their constant chatter was silenced. There were times that he wondered if Bill Collins was real. He questioned if his friend was part of a dream, and wondered if Bill Collins was a figment of his imagination. They carried on conversations. David asked questions, and Bill answered them. The ghosts never answered him. His friend was different from them, not threatening. He brought him food and drink but left him in this prison on the fourth floor. If he was real and if he was a friend, he would take him away from the voices in the vent. After he left, the ghosts would begin talking again and would talk throughout the night. He listened. With time, he began to understand the voices in his head and their plan. They had a plan for Bill Collins, and they had a plan to take control of the fourth floor. The ghosts wanted out of the prison behind the wall that had become their home.

It was the bad ghosts that told him about the other ghosts, the ghosts that occupied the showroom on the fourth floor — the good ghosts. They had control of the floor and were the ones that wouldn't let the bad ghosts out from behind the walls.

It was the first Saturday night after David Morgan began living on the fourth floor that he first saw the good ghosts. He was lying in bed listening to the bad ghosts talk through the vent when suddenly they stopped talking. There was complete silence for a few minutes. Then he saw the light coming underneath the door leading to the showroom. He heard talking, laughter — it sounded like a party. He approached the door, turned the doorknob, and opened it. That's when he saw the crowd of people dressed in colorful clothes from a time long ago. In front of him was the furniture, the crystal chandeliers dangling from the ceiling, the two fireplaces with logs blazing at their base. He saw the bar with people crowded around and the piano player in the corner of the room. Everything looked new, fresh, expensive, and from a time long ago. Then the laughter, the talking, and the music stopped. Everyone stood still, looking at him. One tall, distinguished looking older man approached. When he was ten feet away, he stopped. David Morgan recognized him. It was Thomas Adler, the man he had murdered years earlier. Thomas Adler raised his hand, and a large gust of wind pushed David Morgan back inside the storage room. The door slammed shut and locked. David Morgan was not welcome in the showroom on the fourth floor. He would never be permitted inside that room.

The good ghosts rarely were heard or seen. Mostly they only came out on Saturday nights. Sometimes, on special occasions, they would come out another night. Whenever they did come out, the bad ghosts were silent, he felt safe, and the voices in his head stopped. He was at peace when the good ghosts were present. He had a feeling that, although they didn't like him, they would never harm him.

***

Bill was afraid of the bad ghosts, but he had come to realize that they were locked in their own prison within the hidden room on the fourth floor. After all, he had put them there when he killed them. The security guard believed he was safe from the ghosts as long as he stayed on the other side of the vent. Every night he made trips up the hidden stairway, into the storage room, and into David's room. He delivered food and drinks to David almost every day. He didn't hear the ghosts in the vent when he visited David, but he knew they were there, waiting. It was obvious that the ghosts were talking to his friend. Sometimes, if he were quiet enough when he entered the back room, he could hear David talking to them. David never admitted that he heard the ghosts, but he had pulled his bed right up to the vent so he could listen to them. He talked to himself, and sometimes he talked to the people in the vents. The old man hadn't bathed or changed clothes, even though there was a bathroom with a shower just off his bedroom. The fresh clothes that Bill brought to him hadn't been worn. He hadn't shaved—his beard was long, gray, and dirty. David Morgan was losing touch with reality.

***

Bill had to do something. He had plans for his friend, and he couldn't let him deteriorate beyond help. That's when he decided to tell Dennis Morgan about his father. Dennis had been working at Adler for several months. Since coming home, Dennis had done everything his mother had asked him to do. He had been the perfect son, all in an effort to gain his mother's trust, to earn his rightful place as heir to the Adler fortune. All his suffering, the years at Westminster, the loneliness of having loveless parents had earned him the right of someday soon taking over the Adler business. So naturally, when he told his mother he wanted to enter the business, Dennis assumed he would be given a position in management, possibly as a vice president, just below his mother. Instead, his mother started her son on the ground floor, working in the maintenance department. It was not a job befitting the son of the owner and someone that would someday take over the business. Dennis felt betrayed by his mother. That was when the hate and contempt for his mother began to take hold.

With that job, he worked a lot of late evenings after the store was closed. That's how he met Bill Collins.

When he was told that his father was living on the fourth floor and was going through a difficult time, he wanted to see him. They had a great relationship many years earlier until his mother kicked his father out of the house. In a way, they had gone through some of the same crap. In Dennis's mind, his mother was to blame for all their problems. She had insisted that he go to boarding school. Dennis didn't want that. His father didn't want that for his son either. But what his mother wanted, she got. He didn't blame his father for cheating on his mother. In his mind, his mother treated his father terribly. She deserved what she got. He blamed his mother for kicking his father out of the house. He blamed his mother for the tragic life his father had lived since the divorce. Dennis found hundreds of reasons to blame his mother and no reasons to fault his father. His father had suffered just as he had as a result of his mother.

The night he went up to the fourth floor to see his father was a night he would never forget and one that would determine his future. The boy found his father lying in bed, curled up in almost a fetal position. Dennis barely recognized him. The old man looked like he was near death. It was obvious that his father had given up on life by the odor of urine and body excrements of a man that could no longer take care of himself. The clothes he wore were filthy, and from the smell, it didn't appear that his father had bathed in a long time. He was skin and bones, so thin that bones were showing through his skin, and his father looked as close to death as anyone could be and still be breathing.

Dennis cried when he first saw his father, partly because he hadn't seen him for so long and partly because of the way he had deteriorated. He reached down to touch his father's arm.

David Morgan jumped, startled. "Who are you?" he yelled.

"I'm your son, Dennis."

He just stared back at Dennis as if he were trying to remember. It took a few minutes for his memory of his son to resurface. Once it did, they began a long journey of getting to know each other all over again. Dennis vowed to take care of his father, to get him out of the fourth floor and to make a better life for both of them. David was content having his son back in his life again.

***

The reunion of father and son was even more successful than Bill had hoped. Dennis would be on-board with any plan that benefited his father and hurt his mother. David had a reason to live, to pull back from the brink of insanity. He would get stronger and would become useful to Bill Collins again.

The security guard had plans for both—they would be a means to an end. He had responsibilities to the mob. He had to fulfill those responsibilities, and Dennis and David Morgan could do that for him. Bill Collins also had an end game. He knew the mob would never let him out of their grasp. He had already paid off his debt to them many times over. But they still wanted more—they always wanted more. There were only two ways out of the mob. With the father and son's help, he might just be able to find a third way out, one that didn't require a trip to the cemetery.

For nearly three weeks, since the old man had carried the jewels up to the roof of Adler, Bill had not given the mob any additional credit card or client information. He had nearly been killed by the bad ghosts before, and he had no intention of invading their territory again. The security system at Adler prevented him from carrying customer information out the front door. The shipping and delivery doors were also being monitored. The only option to get Adler property or customer information out of the store was by way of the roof. The only access to the roof was through the hidden room behind the vent on the fourth floor. That was where the bad ghosts lived.

Bill had no choice. If he postponed getting the information to the mob any longer, it would likely result in a prolonged hospital stay, or possibly even worse, so he decided to have David take the information up to the roof. But the request to begin making deliveries to the roof was not well received by the old man. David wanted no part of invading the bad ghosts' territory again. The security guard had anticipated that his friend might resist the idea.

"Listen, David," he said. "I've taken care of you ever since I found you on the streets. I even reunited you with your son. You owe me, buddy."

"You're right," David responded. "Ask me almost any other favor and I'll do it for you, but don't ask me to go through that vent to where the bad ghosts live. They nearly killed me before, and they're even angrier now."

That's when the security guard tried a new approach. "Do it for your son, David. Trust me. I've got a plan that will provide you and your son enough money to live out the rest of your lives in comfort. You both deserve that. Linda has nearly destroyed both of you, and this is your chance to get back at her, to take everything away from her. You and your son deserve what she has kept to herself for so many years. Do what I ask of you now, and I'll be able to give you and Dennis everything you want later."

The lies worked, and suddenly his friend was onboard with whatever he asked of him, even if it meant going into the room of the bad ghosts.

With every trip into their room, the bad ghosts became angrier. They scratched him, flung objects at him, cursed him, and attacked him. The more trips he made to the room, the more violent the attacks were. Deep wounds began appearing on his arms, chest, back, and legs. He knew that with every additional trip through the hidden room, the violence would be worse than the time before, the wounds would be more severe, and the pain would be greater. Bill Collins saw his wounds. He heard his screams and knew the terror David was going through. And eventually, the old man couldn't hide the wounds and pain from his son.

When Dennis discovered the wounds, he confronted Bill and threatened to kill him. He pulled a knife. Bill Collins pulled a gun. David never admitted the existence of the ghosts to his son. Dennis assumed that the security guard had been beating his father. He threatened him and made it clear that he would kill Bill Collins if any more harm came to his father. It was mutually agreed that the old man would not make any more trips to the roof.

Bill would need to find another way to satisfy the Civelli family. A new plan to pay back the mob began to take hold. It was a plan that Bill began formulating the day Linda Adler announced the closing of Adler.

It would be the last job the security guard pulled off for the mob if all went well. He approached Antonio and Anthony Civelli about his plan. There would be one large heist at Adler just before Christmas, when sales were at their highest. Expensive jewelry, cash receipts from the vault, credit card receipts, client files, crystal, and other expensive items would be taken in the theft. The money received from selling the stolen goods and from the receipts in the vault would be split evenly between the Civelli family and Bill Collins. The agreement made was that this would repay Bill Collins's debt to the mob. He would be free of them after this heist. But even though Antonio Civelli promised his freedom, Bill Collins knew differently.

***

Bill enlisted Dennis Morgan to help him with the robbery. It was relatively easy to convince him to rob his mother's store.

His father was edging closer to insanity. His health and his mind were deteriorating rapidly. For all his misery growing up, he never blamed his father. His father was the only person, the only thing in Dennis's life, that he did love. The son had made his father a promise that he would take care of him. The money from the Adler heist would do that. He and his father could start a new life, get to know each other again. The money would solve a lot of problems. The icing on the cake, so to speak, was that it would hurt his mother. Linda Adler would suffer as a result of the robbery. Sure, insurance would take care of most of the financial loss, but her reputation would suffer the most. All of her best client customer files, credit card information, and personal information would have been stolen. Customers that had trusted her for so long would now blame her.

The best part was that she would never suspect Dennis or her ex-husband of being involved in the thefts. Her son planned to stay around long enough to see his mother really suffer. After all, her reputation was everything to her. She would die inside and he could watch his mother deteriorate. Dennis planned to rejoice in her suffering. She was old. Losing her store and her reputation at the same time would surely push her into depression. Maybe her health would be affected. Maybe her mind would be affected. Dennis would play the role of a loving, caring son. He would insist that she see a psychiatrist. Dennis planned to be by her side, to insist that she take whatever pills the doctor gave her. Her son would keep her in a medicated state, and would have her sign an amended will, one that listed him as sole beneficiary. Her suicide would not come as unexpected.

Bill Collins had a plan for the father and son. Dennis had a plan for Bill Collins. Neither wanted to split the profits of the theft. Both wanted to point the finger of the theft at the other one. Both planned to leave Adler that night with all the money.

***

Dennis Morgan knew nothing about the mob's

involvement in the heist. Bill did not share that information with him. He was told that a truck would be parked in the loading dock at the rear of Adler's first floor. The stolen merchandise was to be loaded in the back of the truck. Just before daylight, a driver would drive the truck out of the loading dock and out of town. The merchandise would be fenced by a third party, and within five days, the proceeds from their sales would be split equally between Bill and Dennis. He was not told who the driver was or who would be fencing the merchandise.

The receipts from the safe would be handled differently. Everything in the safe would be put in a black duffle bag, taken up to the fourth floor, and the cash split evenly between the two. This would be done just after the truck carrying the stolen merchandise left the dock. The remaining credit card receipts and personal information of Adler's well-heeled clientele would remain in the duffle bag and would be taken up to the roof. On the roof, near the fire escape, would be a brown duffle bag. That bag would contain twenty thousand in cash, payment for the contents of the black duffle bag. The black duffle bag would be left on the roof and the brown duffle bag would be taken. Dennis Morgan and Bill Collins would get ten thousand dollars each.

Bill Collins also shared his escape plan. After the money had been split, Dennis would follow him downstairs to his office. Once inside, he would hand Dennis an untraceable handgun. With it, he would shoot the security guard in the shoulder, in a place that would not be fatal. He would wipe his fingerprints off the gun and toss it in a dumpster several blocks away from the store after he made his escape off the roof and down the fire escape.

One other thing needed to be done — the surveillance tapes in the security office needed to be destroyed. There could not be any video recordings of the crime. Bill suggested that Dennis set fire to the tapes and all the files in the security room. That would destroy evidence and cover-up the stolen customer files. It would also set off the fire alarm that would alert police, who could arrive before Bill's wound became life-threatening. Dennis was to bring a five-gallon container of gasoline with him that night when he broke into the back door.

Besides omitting the information about the mob being involved in the heist, there were a couple of other pieces of information that Bill Collins omitted. He did not tell Dennis about Connor. Dennis was under the impression that only Bill Collins and his father would be inside Adler the night of the break-in. Secondly, he didn't tell Dennis about the ghosts on the fourth floor, and he was hoping that his father wouldn't tell him either.

Dennis would have some surprises of his own for Old Man Collins. He did not tell him that he was part of a gang of four that would be coming that night. Bill was taken by surprise when he saw four men dressed in black, with face masks and gloves, approach the unlocked back door. Bill had counted on only Dennis being there. He had counted on one video camera, whose tapes would not be destroyed, capturing a picture of Dennis breaking into the back door. The security guard had counted on framing Dennis and his father for the crime. When he saw the four men entering the store, he knew that Dennis had double-crossed him, and that his life was in danger. That's when he decided to kill them before they killed him.

He grabbed his weapon and ran up the stairs to the first floor and back to the storage room. But they heard him coming. They were ready, and they caught him by surprise. As they dragged him back to the basement, Bill knew they planned to kill him. When Dennis asked him if anyone else was in the store, he said no. The security guard knew Dennis would believe him, and he hoped that Connor would find some place to hide or some way to escape. Old Man Collins really did care about Connor, and considered him a friend. That was the only part of his plan for the robbery that bothered him. If his plan went as expected, he would have had to kill Connor. That wasn't something he wanted to do, and he considered several alternate scenarios. There was no way around it. If Bill Collins was to live, Connor would need to die.

CHAPTER 10
CONNOR'S REUNION WITH HIS GRANDFATHER

Ron Caldwell stepped out of the elevator and shook hands with Thomas Adler. Connor watched in amazement. *Is this a dream?* he wondered. His grandfather died when he was six years old. The young Connor had gone to his funeral, said a prayer, and laid the medal down on his casket. His grandfather was dead. Connor knew that. Yet he was looking directly at him now, and the old man looked exactly like Connor remembered. He looked exactly like the picture Grandma Rose had of him in her house. It was impossible. Either Connor was dreaming, or he was looking at a ghost. Maybe he was going insane.

Ron Caldwell turned and looked at his grandson, then raised his hand and motioned for Connor to come to him. Connor just stood there staring back at his grandfather, his legs locked in place. The boy wanted to go to him, but he couldn't. Fear had glued his feet to the floor.

In an instant, Ron Caldwell came to him. So did Thomas Adler. One second ago, they were standing clear across the room. In the next second, they were directly in front of Connor. He raised his hand to touch his grandfather. His hand went through him. The only thing he touched was air.

"Don't be afraid," he said to his grandson. "I was sent here to protect you. I saved your life once at the bottom of the stairway in the basement, but my job isn't done. Once it is, I will be gone, and you will not see me again until someday, many years down the road. Mr. Adler and all the people you see in this room are only temporary residents of this world. We will all leave when our work is done. Think of us as your guardian angels. We are here to protect you because it is not your time to leave this world. The men downstairs know about you. They will be coming for you soon. You must do exactly as I tell you when the time comes."

"Wait, I don't understand. Grandpa, what is going on? I have so many questions for you. Who are the people downstairs? Why do they want to harm me? Who are these people in this room? Are they ghosts? Why are they here? Who are the ghosts behind the walls? Who is the man that hit me over the head and tied me up, the same man that isn't allowed to come into this room?"

"I know you have a lot of questions. There are some things that I can share with you and some things I cannot. I can tell you this much. Our lives are predetermined. Everyone has a certain fate, and no matter what choices we make in life, it will ultimately end in the same fate. Even in death, we have a predetermined fate. We have a role in the afterlife, a job, a responsibility. Death in your world is no more than a steppingstone to another life. My job is to see that your fate is not altered. People like me, guardian angels, if you will, are sent when circumstances are being created that will alter that fate. That is happening to you, and that is why I am here. The people in this room share a common bond. They are here to see that another soul meets the fate that they were predetermined to have. In short, we correct fates that are in danger of being altered.

"The voices you hear behind the walls in the other room are different. You call them ghosts. I would call them lost souls. They have a place to go, but they refuse to accept it. They must be shown the way. Until they leave, they are dangerous. Stay away from them. The man on the other side of the door also has a fate. People are trying to alter it too. He is not what he seems. He cannot be permitted to come into this room until we are ready for him. Do not trust him. There are other people in your life that aren't what they seem. You will discover that soon.

"Connor, we must go now. But know that when you need me, I will be here."

Before Connor could say another word, the fog reappeared. It covered the entire room. In less than a minute, it was gone, and so were the people. The room became pitch black in an instant. Connor opened the door to the other room and entered. David Morgan was waiting.

"Are they going to help me? Are they going to protect me?"

Connor had not lied much in his life. He always felt that it was better to be honest, even if it was painful sometimes. But he lied this time. He remembered what his grandfather had said about David Morgan. "Do not trust him."

Connor said, "Yes, they said that they would protect you when the time comes."

***

David Morgan had a lot of secrets. He had murdered Thomas Adler. He was partly responsible for the murder-suicide on the fourth floor that claimed the lives of Denise and Ron Caldwell. Much of his life had been a lie. It was because of those lies that he found himself on the fourth floor of Adler, trying desperately to survive the night.

He did not marry Linda Adler because he loved her. His dark soul was incapable of such feelings. He knew just about as much about Linda Adler as she knew herself before they even went on their first date. She was his target. She was his winning lottery ticket. It wasn't her that he wanted—it was her money, specifically the Adler family money. The moment they married, Thomas Adler's life was in danger. With him gone, his daughter would inherit everything. That would put David one step closer to inheriting a fortune. The birth of his son, Dennis, delayed his plans. Now there was another Adler in the family, another person that would share in the inheritance. He could not murder both his wife and son and expect to get away with it. He would have to wait and look for the right opportunity.

It didn't take long for Linda and David to realize that their son was different from other children. For one, he never cried, even at birth. His mother laid in bed after giving birth, waiting to hear the first cries of life from her baby boy. There were none. She began to scream in agony, thinking her son was not breathing. "Don't worry," the doctor told her. "He's perfectly healthy, just a little shy." But he never cried—not when he was hungry, not when he had a messy diaper, not even when he was sick. He didn't need the attention of his parents. In fact, he seemed to resist the attention. He was a loner, unable, or possibly incapable of socializing with other children. He played by himself and almost never smiled. When he did smile, it was normally because of someone else's pain. He seemed to relish witnessing pain. Even as a young child, he had a passion for destroying things. Nearly every toy he was given as a young boy was destroyed. If he could tear it apart, he would. If he could disfigure it, he would. As he got older, he began stealing things from the house—mainly knives, tools, or anything sharp or capable of inflicting pain or destruction.

His mother was too busy with the store to realize how dangerous her son was becoming. But her husband knew and recognized the psychotic tendencies in his son. They were many of the same tendencies he had as a youth. In a way, he understood him better than anyone else, and he empathized with him, like father, like son. He thought he could hide his son's dark side from others, much like his parents had hidden David's dark side from others for so many years. But he wasn't about to do to his son what his parents had done to him in an effort to hide his psychotic tendencies from the outside world. They thought the answer was a 6' X 10' room in the cellar, which they called the behavior adjustment room. When David's dark side surfaced, his father would take him down to the cellar and lock him in the room. The boy stayed there like a caged animal, with water and food given to him only once a day. He would stay there on the damp, dirt floor, living among roaches and rats, until his father deemed that the punishment had been appropriate for the crime.

David Morgan was not going to torture his son. He hoped to contain that evil inside his son and keep it from being realized until he could find a way to use it for his own gains. When his son turned his attention from destroying and disfiguring toys to needing to harm living things, he knew the dark side of his son was beginning to take over. For a while, he would feed his son's needs by bringing him insects, frogs, and other small animals to torture.

The basement in the Adler mansion became a sort of torture chamber. No member of the household staff was allowed to go into the basement. Linda never went into it. Hell, she was rarely home, and when she was home, she was only there to sleep. She was oblivious to what her son was becoming. Only David and his son went there. The torture would escalate, and with it, the need for larger animals to torture and kill. Cats became Dennis's favorite victims. They were able to demonstrate fear and voice pain. He felt excitement. His adrenaline popped when he could see and hear their suffering. The woods, a hundred yards behind the Adler mansion, became a graveyard for his victims.

As his son grew, it became more difficult for David to hide his psychotic behavior. When he began attending school, it didn't take long for the other children and the teachers to realize he was different from the others. The young Adler didn't socialize with the other kids. He rarely talked and almost never showed any outward emotion. Pain didn't seem to bother him. Once he stepped on a nail on the playground during recess but said nothing about it. He walked on it, embedding it deeper in his foot. Blood coated his sock and seeped into his shoe and down onto the floor. That's when the teacher noticed it and took him to the nurse's office. From there, he went to the emergency room. The boy never complained and never showed any emotion. No one ever saw Dennis cry. That was an emotion he was incapable of. Other children avoided him. Teachers ignored him. Everyone that met him thought he was odd. But only his father knew how dangerous he was.

Things were about to get worse. His appetite for committing sadistic acts was growing. Torturing cats no longer satisfied his appetite for depravity. He started bringing stray dogs home to the basement. The sounds of their suffering echoed through the thick concrete walls of the basement and into the house. The house staff was becoming aware of the torture going on in the basement — several left. Finding replacements became difficult.

One house staff member that wasn't frightened away was Diane Perry. It took a lot to frighten her, and she certainly wasn't afraid of a seven-year-old boy or his drunk, philandering father. Diane was an outspoken black woman that had grown-up in the racist south before the Civil Rights Movement. Her family moved to the north after Martin Luther King was murdered. She had seen more death, cruelty, and hatred as a youth than most people experienced during their entire lifetime. The staff had been told that no one was allowed to go into the basement, but that wasn't going to stop her. She was a strong-willed woman. Diane knew something sinister was going on in that basement and was also confident that whatever was going on, Linda Adler knew nothing about it. Diane admired Mrs. Adler. Like her, she was another strong-willed woman. She didn't depend on a man to take care of her. Diane shared that characteristic with her employer. Her husband, a drunk and philanderer much like Mr. Morgan, had left her for a younger woman ten-years earlier. Diane learned to take care of herself.

The inquisitive nature in her convinced Diane that

she needed to know what was going on downstairs. If it was something sinister, and she suspected it was, she would alert Linda Adler. She could have called the police with her suspicions, but that wouldn't benefit her or her employer. No, it was better to keep things quiet, discover for herself what was down in the basement, and report what she saw to Mrs. Adler. Her boss would appreciate the discretion, and Diane would very likely be rewarded for it. Diane had bigger aspirations than being a housekeeper. Perhaps by helping Linda Adler, she would be rewarded with a position in her store.

Her opportunity to see what was in the basement came on a stormy Thursday evening. Linda was working late, as usual. David and Dennis had left the house. Diane wasn't sure, but she thought they were going to dinner, as they often did on Thursday evenings. Five minutes after their car pulled out of the driveway, Diane headed toward the steps leading to the basement. Then she suddenly stopped. The basement door would be locked. It was always locked. She had once spied on Mr. Morgan when he placed a key on a hook behind a bottle of Old Crow in his liquor cabinet in the den. Could it be possible that was a key that would open the basement door?

She walked to the door leading into the den. It was unlocked. She opened it and walked in. The room was dark. The window shades had been shut, but even if they hadn't, the room would be just as dark. Dark rain clouds had rolled in, and it was eerily dark outside for this time of day. Rain was coming down heavier now, and the only light outside was an occasional bolt of lightning in the distance.

The maid opened the liquor cabinet directly behind Mr. Morgan's antique oak desk. The bottle of Old Crow was on the third shelf of the cabinet, too high for Diane Perry's tiny 5'2" frame. She grabbed a chair sitting in front of the desk, positioned it directly underneath the cabinet, and stepped on top of the seat. Even with the aid of the chair, she could barely reach the bottle of Old Crow. Diane lifted her right hand to move the bottle just enough to expose the key hanging on a hook behind it. For the additional few inches that were needed to reach the key, she stood on her toes on the seat of the chair, stretched her right hand and fingers as far as they would go, and with just a slight bounce of her toes off the chair, she pulled the key off the hook. That was when she saw the flash of lightning just fractions of a second before it collided with the ground just outside the window, causing a deafening sound of thunder that caused her to lose her balance. Her arms collided with several bottles of fine Kentucky bourbon. One tipped, resulting in several others falling to the floor and shattering.

Diane tried to keep her balance, but it was no use. The chair wobbled underneath her, and her body fell awkwardly off the right side of the chair as it toppled over on top of her. Some of the pieces of glass from the broken bottles cut into her back, arms, and legs as she landed back first on the floor. Other than a few minor cuts, she was not hurt. She smelled like a brewery, though. Her back had landed in a puddle of bourbon from the broken bottles. The mess was going to be impossible to hide or to explain to David Morgan. With a little luck, she would be gone by the time he and Dennis arrived back home. Maybe then, she wouldn't need to explain it. She could say that she had left before the accident happened. Maybe he would think the storm caused the accident. After all, that lightning striking right outside the window did shake the house. "Who's to say that the shaking of the house couldn't have caused the liquor bottles to fall?" she convinced herself. The maid moved the chair back into place and wiped the bourbon off it.

Diane considered putting the key back and leaving the house. She had already created a big enough problem for herself. If Mr. Morgan suspected that she had gone into his den and opened the liquor cabinet to remove the key, he would fire her on the spot. And without evidence of what he and his son had been doing in the basement, Mrs. Adler would not stand up for her. So, she was convinced that she needed that evidence. For that, she would have to go into the basement.

Diane hurried to the basement door, inserted the key, and it opened. She smiled. At least the mess she had created in the den wasn't for nothing. The key in the liquor cabinet had worked. The musty, damp smell of the basement was a bit nauseating. She covered her nose and mouth with her left hand, turned on the basement light just to the right of the stairs, and started down.

The stairs were old, wooden, and in need of repair. They creaked with every step. Several bowed just slightly as her feet, then her tiny frame pressed against them—fifteen steps to the bottom—a rather steep descent. The old mansion was built before the turn of the century, before refrigeration. The basement was built deep with high ceilings to take advantage of the cool earth. In those days, food that needed to be kept cool was stored down there. Floor to ceiling measured fifteen feet. It was a large cavern of a room. She could feel the temperature cool more with every step she took. The light at the top of the steps only illuminated a small portion of the basement directly in front of her. There would be more light switches to turn on when she reached the basement.

At the foot of the stairs, she heard the pounding of rain against the basement window. She could see the flashes of lightning reflecting off the basement walls from the two windows on each side of the basement. Thunder roared closer and closer within fractions of a second after the lightning glowed through the windows. She remembered what her daddy had told her about lightning when she was young.

The closer the sound of thunder is to the flash of lightning, indicates how close the lightning is to you.

Based on the quickness of the sound of thunder from the time the flash of lightning occurred, it appeared to Diane that the lightning was striking just outside the window.

On the wall to the right of the base of the stairs was the second light switch. She turned it on. It illuminated about a third of the basement area. She stopped and looked around for anything out of the ordinary. A workbench was in one corner with tools hanging on the wall above it. A shelf containing paint, turpentine, paint rollers, and brushes was against another wall. There was nothing unusual.

A flash of light and a loud boom of lightning, occurring almost simultaneously, shook the shelves and made Diane jump. *That was too close,* she thought to herself. The maid took a deep breath of courage and moved farther into the basement, stopping at the second light switch. She hesitated for a second before turning it on, allowing her to gather her nerve and prepare for what she might see. After taking in another long, deep breath, she turned the light on.

The light illuminated most of the basement now. There were more shelves containing storage containers, boxes, and odds and ends. All appeared to be organized. There was no clutter. On the far end of the wall, she could see what looked like a large sink with a workbench just a few feet away. Both were just inside the shadows at the edge of the light. They were difficult to see.

It was in the area of the second basement light that Diane's nose began to burn just slightly. There was a strong smell of ammonia coming up from the basement floor, penetrating her nostrils and causing a slight burning sensation. She covered her face with her left hand to soften the burn. The floor was spotless, as if it had been freshly cleaned. Diane moved closer toward the sink and workbench on the other side of the room. As she did, the smell of bleach or ammonia became more pugnacious. She took slower, more shallow breaths underneath her hand to soften the burning sensation in her nose and now rolling into her eyes. Tears began to slide down her cheeks from the water building up in her eyes. As the tears welled up in her eyes, she found it difficult to see anything in front of her. She wiped them with the sleeve of her navy-blue top. That helped, but only for a few seconds. The tears were rolling steadily down her cheeks now.

She moved to the final light switch. When she turned it on, every area of the basement would be visible to her. Another bolt of lightning struck, causing the floorboards above her to shake and the lights to flicker. "God, don't let the lights go out, not now, I beg you," she said in a low voice, looking up to the ceiling. Another flash of light from a lightning bolt came through the basement windows, followed by a roar of thunder. The light illuminated the back of the basement for a brief second, just long enough for Diane to get a glimpse of the sink. It looked pink. She was puzzled. Either her eyes were playing tricks on her, or perhaps the flash of orange and yellow light from the lightning hitting the sink just right in the shadows caused it to look pink.

Again she took a deep breath before turning on the last light. When the light came on, she wiped her eyes one more time with her sleeve and then focused her attention on the rear wall and the area around the sink. She took two steps toward the sink before her eyes focused, and she could clearly see ahead of her. That's when she let out a scream, and chills ran through her body. The sink next to the workbench wasn't pink after all. It was red. The inside of the basin and part of the outside was covered in dried blood. The workbench to its right was covered in plastic, also coated in dried blood. Several tools—a hammer, a screwdriver, pliers, and a wrench—were laying on the table, coated in blood. She was right. Horrible things had gone on in the basement.

She could have turned around then. She could have called Mrs. Adler. She would come home. Diane could take her in the basement and show her what had been going on behind her back. For a brief second, that was what she decided to do. Then she saw the door just on the other side of the workbench. Maybe the truth of what the father and son had been doing in the basement was behind that door. Her curiosity got the best of her. Diane had to see what was behind that door.

There was another room. The door was shut, but light was penetrating underneath the door frame. She listened for any movement but could hear nothing except the sound of the rain bouncing off the basement windows. *Someone must have left the light on,* she thought. She focused her attention away from the sink and workbench and moved to the door. Whatever sick, deviant acts the father and son had been doing in the basement must be behind that door, she thought. Slowly and quietly, she turned the knob on the door. It wasn't locked. Behind that door, she would have proof of what Mr. Morgan and his son had been up to in the basement for so long. With that proof, she could go to Mrs. Adler. With that proof, she could better her lot in life.

The door was made of solid, thick wood — it took all her strength to push it open. Inside, the room wasn't what she thought it was. It was tiny. It appeared to be a small bathroom. A hand sink was on one side of the wall. A small, gray hand towel was hanging next to the sink. Its walls were plain, unpainted. One light bulb dangled from the ceiling with a pull cord. That light was on, but it was dim. A strong odor of bleach made her eyes water and her nose itch.

At the back of the room was what looked like a toilet lid on the floor. Around it, the concrete floor looked like it had been removed, exposing a dirt floor. The dirt floor around the toilet lid was dark and damp. There was an odor, different from the bleach smell, coming from the area around the toilet seat. A strong stench of decay was much worse than the smell of bleach. It was much different too. It didn't burn her eyes like the bleach had. Instead, it made her sick to her stomach. *It must be coming from the toilet,* she thought.

Diane had grown up in the south, in poverty. She had seen and used many outhouses in her time. This room reminded her of one of those outhouses. She had seen toilets in those outhouses that were close to the ground. There would be a hole dug deep underneath the toilet seat to gather the feces. The smell would be terrible. They typically used lye to soak up some of the smell, but it only helped a little. The smell was intense. But the odor coming from below this toilet seat was different—it was much worse. She needed to know what was below that toilet seat, what was in the hole in the ground, what was causing that terrible smell.

She held her nose with one hand and lifted the toilet lid with the other. There appeared to be a large, deep hole in the ground. The odor intensified once the lid was removed. Diane stared down into the dark hole, trying to see what was causing the smell, but her eyes were watering, her sight clouded. She wiped her eyes one more time with the sleeve of her blouse, then closed her eyes for a brief second and reopened them, allowing just enough time for her eyes to adjust. There was something down there. She could make out an outline. She bent farther down.

That's when she saw it. The severed head of a dog, a large breed dog, floating in a liquid solution less than five feet from her face.

She screamed and turned to run. A bolt of lightning hit just outside the window. With a flash and a loud boom, the lights in the basement flickered once and then went out. Diane was completely in the dark.

Her body was nearly frozen with fear. She had never liked the dark. Nothing good ever happened in the dark. When she was young, growing up in a housing project in one of the most crime-infested parts of Atlanta, the night was something to be fearful of. After the sun went down was when the gangs and the criminals took over the streets. It was a time to lock and bar the doors and stay inside.

Stuck in the dark basement of two psychopaths with only one exit was not the place she wanted to be. Diane forced her body to move toward the exit, stepping slowly and quietly as she went. The only light to guide her way was an occasional bolt of lightning that glowed through the basement windows. The rain was still pounding against them, causing a loud clatter that echoed in her ears. *They will be coming home soon*, she thought. She had to hurry.

With every flash of lightning that illuminated her way, she picked up her pace. She stopped about ten feet away from the stairs, waiting for another flash of lightning to guide her the rest of the way. That's when she heard it. A different sound than the pounding rain. It sounded like footsteps. She tried to quiet her breathing and listen. The sound stopped. *It must be my mind playing tricks*, she reasoned.

Another glow of lightning shot through the windows, and she saw him standing at the bottom of the stairs. Diane was crippled with fear, unable to scream. She was too petrified to move. Diane Perry became Dennis Morgan's first human victim. She would spend the next several days chained up in the small room at the back of the basement. Her death would be slow and painful. Her gagged mouth and the insulated walls of that basement would soften her screams. The disturbed son and father would take their time to dismember her, starting with smaller, less vital parts of her body and even tending to her wounds to prolong her life. Diane would wish that they had killed her on the first day. Her final resting place would be in the woods behind the mansion in a shallow grave amongst many smaller shallow graves.

CHAPTER 11
NURTURING THE DARK SIDE

Linda Adler and her son would need to be dead for David Morgan to inherit the entire Adler estate. That was still his plan. But with any murder, there is always the chance of getting caught. If he could get Dennis to murder his mother, and through his own negligence, got caught, that would solve all of his problems. Dennis was almost psychopathic enough to do it. His father just needed to nurture the dark side of his son a little longer. He was not quite ready to murder on his own. The killing of Diane Perry had put him on the edge of the psychotic cliff, but he wasn't quite ready to jump. David needed to push him over.

His son enjoyed inflicting pain and enjoyed watching his victims suffer. The several days he tortured the maid in the basement had pushed his dark side to a new level. Dennis had never tortured a person before. In the past, his victims had always been animals. The thrill he experienced from inflicting pain on her was more intense than anything he had done before. The crazed son would never go back to torturing animals. Humans would be his new target. Still, he had not killed a person. Even with Diane, his passion was inflicting pain. He enjoyed hearing her suffer. Killing her ended that suffering and ended the thrill he had been experiencing. His father had to step in and ended her life. David had a tiny amount of compassion. His son did not. "There is only so much pain you can put someone through," he told Dennis. "When their will to live is gone, you must put them out of their misery."

The father was a mentor to his son. David helped him find an outlet for his dark side, and at the same time, was able to feed his own demons. When he thought his son was ready to kill, he drove him to an abandoned warehouse a few blocks from the Plaza area and the Adler store. The building was the home for a number of homeless people trying to avoid sleeping in the streets. David Morgan had been there before. It was a fertile hunting ground for victims that nobody cared about. This time was different, though. David was hunting for the perfect victim for his son. He needed a victim that would push his son's boundaries. His son needed someone that would fight back. With his past victims, Dennis had always been the aggressor. He had never been threatened by one of his victims before. David had seen how angry his son could get and had seen the darkness in his eyes, the redness in his face, the tightening of his fists. But he had never been pushed far enough to kill. Tonight would be different.

The abandoned warehouse that David chose for his hunting ground had been home to a gun manufacturer nearly twenty years earlier. A fire in the factory on the lower two floors had gutted the lower levels. Smoke damage crippled the remaining five floors of the old brick building. Arson was the suspected cause of the fire that happened in the wee hours on a Sunday morning. No one was in the building at the time of the blaze. At the time of the fire, the employees of the Arlington Rifle Company, owners of the building, were on strike. Their union had called for a strike nearly six months earlier. Picket lines, peaceful during the early days of the strike, had turned more aggressive in recent weeks when the manufacturer began interviewing and hiring non-union help in an attempt to reopen the factory. The owners blamed the union for the fire, but no one was ever charged with the arson. With an aging factory, high labor costs, and the expense of rebuilding the factory after the fire, the owners decided to close the factory and move their operations elsewhere. The factory had been vacant ever since.

The building, deteriorating from neglect, had become a housing refuge for the area's homeless. It was safer and offered more protection against the harsh Kansas City winters and hot, humid summers than living on the street. Besides, the police left its residents alone. Out of sight, out of mind, so to speak.

A normal person would take one look at the large, dark building, with its broken windows and crumbling façade, and they would turn around and leave. The building was intimidating, especially at night. There were no lights. The abandoned building was isolated from the street and from civilization. Hidden from view, it sat at the rear of a large, concrete parking lot, surrounded by a ten-foot chain-link fence, weathered from time and neglect, which provided the only obstacle to getting inside. But that fence had plenty of broken sections and was falling in several areas where its residents and people with ill intentions had toppled it to get inside. The entire parking lot was cracked due to weather and weeds that had penetrated the surface from the moist ground below. Some areas of the parking lot were so overgrown with weeds and small bushes and trees that had grown up from the ground that it looked more like a forest than a parking lot.

David parked just outside the fence. He and Dennis maneuvered past the fence and into the weed infested parking lot. Both carried flashlights to guide their way. Insects feasting off the waist deep weeds bit at their legs and arms. There was a full moon out that night, which provided some light, but the flashlights were helpful in the areas where the brush was so high and dense that it clouded the moonlight. Twenty minutes into their walk, they reached the building. The first door they tried was jammed. But, with an abundance of shattered windows at the ground level and one section of the wall that had partially caved in, there was no problem getting inside.

A fire many years earlier had destroyed much of the interior of the first floor. It was completely littered with debris. Wood pillars were charred. The ceiling had partially collapsed, creating a large opening that exposed a portion of the second floor. Wood walls and insulation behind them had burned, exposing the outer brick wall. The fire had charred the inside of the bricks but had not penetrated them. Broken glass covered the perimeter of the room. The smell of burning wood had long since disappeared, but the evidence of the fire's intensity and destruction was all around.

At the back of the room was a thick, metal fire door. On the other side of it was a staircase leading up to the other floors. The fire had not penetrated the metal door, and the staircase on the other side was in reasonably good shape. They ascended the staircase past the second floor, past the third floor, past the fourth floor, past the fifth floor, past the sixth floor, to the top floor. Most of the vagrants slept on the third floor. At least that had been David Morgan's experience during his previous trips to the building. The type of victim suitable for his son's needs would most likely be found on an upper level of the building, isolated and not fearful of being alone. They would be independent. They would have some fight left in them.

The seventh floor of the building was hauntingly quiet. The light from their flashlights illuminated the way past large wooden shelves containing boxes of all sizes and shapes. Most were torn or turned over, many laying on the ground, most likely the result of past scavengers going through them looking for anything of value. *This must have been a storage room before the fire,* thought David.

Dennis followed a few steps behind his father as they moved slowly past the empty boxes and trash covering most of the concrete floor. Dennis had always admired and looked up to his father. Recently, he had learned to depend on him to feed his lust for violence. He wouldn't have had Diane Perry to torture if it wasn't for his father. The father had been aware of his son's needs for a long time. David set up the basement to accommodate his son's urges. For the last couple of years, he had helped his son scavenge for small animals to use in his torture and had helped him bury the evidence in the woods behind the mansion. He even designed the disposal hole that was located in the small room in the basement. It was the perfect place to dispose of larger carcasses that could not easily be carried into the woods and buried. It took him nearly two weeks to hammer out the concrete floor and dig a large enough hole. Then he had to find a large barrel made from a metal component that would not corrode from the hydrofluoric acid that would be used to eat the flesh and bones dropped into the hole. The first time the hole was used was a learning experiment. Dennis's latest torture victim was a large breed dog found wandering the neighborhood a few blocks away. The dog was a mixed breed, part hound dog, part lab, David figured. When Dennis was done with the dog it was nearly dead and had lost any will to live. David put it out of its misery. The carcass must have weighed eighty pounds, too heavy to carry all the way to the woods. So David dragged what remained of the dog into the small room next to his workbench. He and his son lifted the carcass over the hole and dropped it in. They filled the hole partially with water, then filled it most of the rest of the way with hydrofluoric acid. The smell was horrendous. The acid penetrated the dog's skin and emitted an odor that shot through the entire basement. Plenty of bleach and a layer of a strong ammonia-based floor cleaning solution helped mask the smell. The animal carcass was still partially intact, floating at the top of the liquid solution when Diane Perry decided to look inside the hole.

Diane's remains became a positive cycle of learning for her killers. They needed to dispose of her body, but they could neither carry her into the woods nor dump her body into the hole without some alterations. Her entire body would not easily dissolve in the hole. David decided to invest in two pieces of equipment to help in his disposal process. First, he purchased a high-quality chain saw. Then he purchased a top-quality wood chipper. He used the chainsaw to cut the maid into manageable pieces. Then he placed the wood chipper at the far end of his back yard just before the woods. He carried the pieces of his victim, in several plastic bags, out to the woodchipper and put them in, one bag at a time. His disposal problem was solved, although he did not count on the amount of blood and pieces of flesh that would fly out of the machine as it ground down her bones. The clothes he was wearing that day would need to be burned.

Dennis trusted his father. They both had secrets that only the other one knew about. Besides, his father was his mentor. He had his son's best interest in mind. David knew his son's hunger for depravity could not be stopped. So he chose to embrace it, feed it, help it grow. After all, his son was much like him, and David had learned to live among the normal people without being discovered for what he was.

Dennis followed his father on this adventure with the excitement of a young boy going to shop for a new toy. That night they would spot what David was looking for at a far corner of the room. There, arched like a caged animal, ready to strike at anyone or anything that came between her and an escape route off the seventh floor, was a young woman, a blanket still covering the lower portion of her body. Emily Potts had been asleep on the floor in the corner of the room, underneath an open window, when she heard the two strangers walking into the room between her and the stairway. It was the only escape route off the seventh floor. She waited quietly in the corner of the room, trying to blend into her dark surroundings, hoping that the strangers wouldn't notice her. In her right hand, she held a large, thick piece of wood that she could use to defend herself if needed.

David knew when he saw her that she would be the perfect victim for his son to cross the boundary between torture and murder. She had the look of a cornered, rabid animal. Emily would not die without putting up a fight. A fight was exactly what his son needed for his anger to take control. It was that anger, his father reasoned, that would push him to commit his first murder. So, with his son just a few feet behind him, David took the initiative to toy with his victim. He moved within a few feet of her, and she recoiled like a rattlesnake ready to strike.

"Do you know what we are here for?" he asked the woman with a sinister looking smile on his face.

"No," she said with a defiant tone to her voice.

"We've come here to kill you," he said.

Emily Potts reacted to that statement exactly the way the father had hoped she would. She lunged from her spot on the floor, her crude, wood weapon raised and came directly toward him. She was a tiny framed woman. He could have swatted her away, pulled the knife he had in his right pocket, and finished her right there. But instead, he moved quickly out of her way, leaving a clear path to the stairway, with only his son standing between her and escape. Dennis did not move. She wielded her wood weapon and struck Dennis across his left arm and shoulder. The force of the blow knocked him to the floor. Before she could strike a second blow, David stepped behind her, wrapped his arms around her neck, and forced her to the floor. "Finish her, son," he yelled at Dennis.

David Morgan watched as the anger rose on his son's face. Dennis had never been hit before. He was always the hunter, never the hunted. He was reacting to the attack on him exactly the way his father thought he would. Anger was taking control of him. His eyes were dark and distant as if a demon had possessed him. He did not make the victim suffer for very long. His motivation that night was not to inflict pain but instead to take a life. His anger had pushed him over the edge. The homeless woman became Dennis Morgan's first murder victim.

That night, Dennis had made his father very proud. It

was a giant step for his son, going from a person that enjoyed inflicting pain to becoming a cold-blooded murderer. He was so young, much younger than David had been the first time he took a life. His son's demons were growing even faster than he anticipated. Soon, murder would become second nature to him. It would become as easy and natural as breathing. It was only a matter of time before he would be ready to murder his mother. David knew the trigger that would push his son to murder. When the time was right, he was sure he could create the circumstances that would result in Linda Adler provoking her son into killing her. Then, with his wife gone and his son in prison, the Adler estate would be all his.

David was in a particularly good mood driving home that night. His son, covered in blood from the night's activities, sat quietly, staring straight ahead. *The demons haven't completely left his body*, his father reasoned. It would take a while. Until then, he would be in a world by himself, a state of purgatory somewhere between sanity and insanity.

The moon was full, and a cool breeze was blowing from the north. David turned on the radio, rolled down the windows, and took in the fresh air on his drive home. The first sign of trouble came when he pulled into the driveway of the Adler mansion. Parked in front of the garage was his wife's car. He didn't expect her to be home. She was scheduled to be out of town on a buying trip. Most likely, she was asleep—it was early in the morning. David stopped the car at the bottom of the driveway and turned the engine off. He needed a minute to think. It was nearly five.

"Dennis, your mother may be awake. She must not see you like this. I need you to go in the house through the basement. Quietly go up the rear stairs to your bedroom. Get out of those clothes. Hide them under the bed. Change into your pajamas and get under the covers until she leaves for work. Will you do exactly as I say?"

"Yes"

So far, David had been successful in hiding his son's dark side from his wife. He wasn't ready for her to find out now. David had a different plan for himself. He would leave, drive around, and come back later in the morning after his wife had left for work. She would, most likely, never know that he was gone. For weeks, since their last fight, they had slept in separate bedrooms. Spending time in another bedroom was becoming routine for him. His wife would suspect him of cheating, normally with good merit. They would argue, and she would throw him out of her bedroom. Normally, his punishment would only last a day or two. Usually, she would forgive him. But not this last time. It had been almost three weeks since he was sent to another room. Over that period of time, they had only spoken a handful of times. *She was really pissed this time*, he told himself. He knew that eventually, she would forgive him, and he would once again be allowed in her bed. She loved him. He knew that. He was like an addiction to her. She had tried numerous times over the years to break herself of that addiction, but she always went back to him.

He watched his son walk up the driveway and around to the back of the house, where the basement entrance was located. Then he started the engine, backed out of the driveway, and sped away. The next three hours would be spent at a small neighborhood bar in the central west end of town. He ordered a hearty breakfast of bacon, eggs, and hash browns and chased the meal down with three Bloody Marys.

It was when he got back home at a few minutes past eight-thirty that he realized how poorly his plan had gone. Linda was waiting for her husband. She hadn't gone into work that morning. Something terrible had happened, and she was visibly upset. Tears were streaming down her face.

"We need to do something. We need to do something right away," she screamed at her husband through her tears.

At first, David thought that she was upset with him. Most likely, she had not forgiven him over the last fling that landed him in a separate bedroom. Now, he had been caught out all night and was certain she was about to threaten to kick him out of the house. David braced himself for her temper to erupt from behind those tears. She had always thrown a tantrum when she suspected another one of his indiscretions. The tantum would normally be followed by a barrage of cursing, a little pushing, and a slap to his face before she stormed off. He prepared himself for that.

But it wasn't her husband that she was upset with. His wife didn't even seem to care that he had been gone all night or that he had liquor on his breath. Linda had caught her son sneaking into the house. She'd seen his blood covered clothes and witnessed the darkness in his eyes.

The door to the basement had been dead-bolted from the inside. David had forgotten to give his son the key to that second lock, so Dennis was forced to go around to the front of the house to get inside. His mother saw him enter the house.

Linda did not know the extent of her son's depravity. He refused to talk to her. She only knew what she saw, and what she saw frightened the crap out of her. Linda Adler was concerned, but not so much for her son — she was concerned that her reputation could be tarnished. People might find out about Dennis, and if they did, it would be a reflection on her. People always blamed the parents for the crimes of their children. Linda Adler decided that morning, before she had confronted her husband, that her son must go. She would find him a boarding school, far away, that specialized in working with troubled youth. Maybe they could help him.

David tried to talk his wife out of sending her son away. That would disrupt his plans. But it was no use — Linda Adler's mind was made up. A few days later, Dennis was sent off to Westminster.

David delayed his plans for his wife. He had no choice. With Dennis gone, there was no foolproof way to dispose of his wife without the chance of getting caught. Besides, there was no rush. Linda had forgiven her husband again. He was back in her good graces and back in her bed. His life was comfortable again. His wife loved him so much that she refused to acknowledge many of her husband's weaknesses. Her husband cheated on her, gambled, drank too much, and for the most part, she always forgave him. David was a scoundrel.

Linda Adler knew that, but she still forgave him, at least for a while. But when rumors of another mistress in her husband's life surfaced, she could not ignore his philandering any longer. This time the rumors involved her husband and a young salesclerk at her store. She had turned her back on her husband's extra-marital affairs before, but not this time. This time, her husband had crossed the line. This time he had the nerve to have an affair with one of his wife's employees. It wouldn't take long for knowledge of the affair to spread throughout the store. Linda could not allow that to happen. After all, she had an impeccable reputation.

Linda Adler prepared for divorce, but it needed to be on her terms. He could not be allowed to walk away with even a penny of the Adler estate. He needed to be humiliated. His reputation needed to be destroyed. She hired a private investigator, an ex-member of the Kansas City police force, someone that came highly recommended to her. His name was Bill Collins.

***

The private investigator followed David Morgan the night of his rendezvous with Denise Caldwell. He witnessed everything that happened that night and took photographs of the two of them in a compromising state. When Ron Caldwell entered the store holding the gun, the private investigator could have stoned him. The old man was fragile. His hands were shaking. Bill could have prevented what happened that night. Instead, he chose to let everything play out. Stopping the crime wasn't in his best interest. It would have been better for him if David Morgan was not around. Bill waited on the first floor and listened. When he heard the gunshots, he thought Linda's husband was dead. That was his best-case scenario. He left the store, drove a few blocks away, and waited. When the police radio asked for assistance to the Adler store, Bill Collins was the first to arrive, surprised to find David Morgan still alive. That's when his plans changed. The police officer moonlighting as a private detective decided to play both sides of the fence, just like he had with the mob. He would help both David and Linda Adler. That way, he would earn their trust and use that trust to accomplish what he wanted from both of them.

***

David was only a few days away from getting rid of his wife. His plan was about to come to fruition. He would have inherited everything. But because of that fateful night, he would end up with nothing. Sure, he got a divorce settlement, but it was a small fraction of what he would have inherited if his plans had succeeded. As it was, he squandered the money he did get in a very short period of time. Dennis became the key to his future. There is an old saying, "the apple doesn't fall far from the tree," and that was certainly true with Dennis. He was every bit as cold, self-centered, and psychologically unbalanced as his father. He was incapable of love, of any emotion. David saw that in his son at the age of four. That's when he first saw him experiment with torturing animals—frogs at first, then cats and finally dogs. His son had no remorse for his sick acts. The young boy enjoyed watching the animals suffer. It was only a matter of time before he lost total control of what was right and what was wrong. The young Morgan was becoming a psychopath just like his father. Linda had no clue for a long time. Adler was her first love. Her family came in a distant second. She spent very little time around Dennis. He avoided her as much as possible. David Morgan knew about his son's degenerate activities. He covered most of them up. But as he got older, his psychopathic tendencies became more pronounced. David Morgan had spent a lot of time visiting his son at Westminster. He had convinced his son that only he loved him. The father convinced his son that they had to take care of each other because no one else would. His mother needed to be eliminated to set both of them free. The murder would be carried out during the Christmas holiday. That's when Dennis would visit his mother on his winter break.

David's plan to get rid of his wife was only a few days from fruition when he planned the rendezvous with Denise Caldwell. She was no more than another notch in his bedpost. The cheating husband never considered that his lover's jealous husband might interrupt them and destroy all his plans. He was lucky to escape alive that night. But the evening would cost him his marriage and the opportunity to inherit the Adler fortune. David had many years to wonder how Ron Caldwell knew that he and his wife were meeting that night on the fourth floor of Adler. He also wondered how he got into the store. David Caldwell was certain that he had locked the door after entering. Then there was the elevator leading to the fourth floor. It was a private elevator. It took a special key to operate. "How did Ron Caldwell get the key? He should have never been able to get to the fourth floor," he told himself. Then there was the question of the gun. "Why was Ron Caldwell carrying a loaded gun up to the fourth floor? His wife never mentioned that he might be a threat." David was convinced that his lover didn't even know her husband owned a gun.

He wondered about that night and the cover-up that followed. It was just too convenient. A murder-suicide like what happened that night would have been a top news story the following day anywhere else. Even his ex-wife didn't have enough pull to cover-up something like that. David was convinced that Bill Collins was involved. But even he didn't have enough pull to cover-up something that scandalous.

CHAPTER 12
THE BAD BOYS OF WESTMINSTER

Inside the brick walls of Westminster, life was akin to prison. The ten-foot-high iron fence that surrounded the campus was designed to isolate its problems from the outside world. Life inside was strict and regimented. No one cared about its residents. They were troubled, they were disappointments, they were unloved. The primary purpose of Westminster was to break the spirits of its young students to get them to conform to the normality of society. They used a variety of forms of discipline to achieve those goals.

The day Dennis arrived on the campus of Westminster, he was full of spirit. Every boy was full of spirit when they first arrived. It was headmistress Nancy Baczenas' job to break that spirit. The spinster in her early seventies relished her job. She had been the headmistress at Westminster for thirty-two years. A short, tiny-framed, gray-haired woman with piercing brown eyes looked more like a grandmother than a headmistress. Her life was Westminster. It had been ever since she first arrived fresh out of college, fifty-one years earlier. Nancy never married, never even dated during all those years at Westminster. She had been in love once, during her days at Boston College. Reginald P. Ashworth III was a starting linebacker on the Boston College football team. They were a curious looking couple, him 6'5" and 270 lbs., her barely five-foot and thin as a rail. They met in the college library. She spent a lot of time there, studying and reading. He was there to study for a final exam that would mean the difference between passing and failing a class. Nancy loved the classics, anything written by Jane Austen, Charles Dickens, or J.D. Salinger. He hadn't read anything deeper than the sports page of the Boston Globe. They were an odd couple.

She fell in love with his smile, his wavy blond hair, his blue eyes, and his sense of humor. For him, she was different from any woman he had ever dated — she was intelligent, witty, and more mature. But to be fair, most of Reginald P. Ashworth's other dates had been cheerleaders or women with questionable morals. He had always cared more about getting them in bed than about carrying on a deep conversation with them. Nancy Baczenas entered his life at exactly the right time to foster love. They were both seniors. He would be starting a career in his father's bank after graduation. She would make a fine, respectable wife, someone his father and mother would approve of. When he left for Christmas break, he brought Nancy to Long Island with him to meet his parents. It was beautiful there during the Christmas season. Beautiful white snow blanketed the landscape and clung to the branches of the big oak trees. The Ashworth family lived in a large, three-story brick home that overlooked the Atlantic. It was the perfect place and the perfect time to nurture their love affair. With his father and mother's blessing, he proposed to Nancy on Christmas Eve. They had only known each other for thirty-eight days. She was in love with him. He was in love with the way she presented herself.

Their wedding was planned for early June, two weeks after graduation. But staying faithful to his fiancée for six months became too much of a challenge for Reginald P. Ashworth III. He was a man with needs — he needed the love of many women. He had never been faithful to one woman for more than a few weeks. He managed to stay faithful to Nancy for nearly five-months. But when the temptation became too great, he succumbed to his lust. Nancy forgave him the first time, but not the second. She gave Reginald back her engagement ring, took a position with Westminster, and left on a train, broken-hearted, one week after graduation. She vowed on the train ride that she would never let a man hurt her again, and she had been true to that vow for fifty-one years.

Over the years, the inside of Westminster had become as sterile and cold as its headmistress's heart. Its walls were painted a depressing shade of gray. The floors were linoleum, dulling from the years but spotlessly clean. Lighting was soft, and the walls were bare. Thick oak wood doors led to each classroom on the first and second floors. The third floor contained the administrative offices, and the fourth floor contained the living quarters for the staff. Students were housed on the upper floors, five through eight. From the outside, Westminster looked welcoming, with a strong, brick façade stretching eight stories tall and a grand entranceway. It gave a feeling of hope, a feeling of security.

But on the inside, it was reminiscent of a reformatory. Westminster was a boys' boarding school. Other than members of its staff, there were no women.

Dennis was assigned to dormitory room 713. Westminster had a total of sixty dormitory rooms on four floors. Students were assigned a room that contained other students of about the same age and similar backgrounds. Each room, or "housing unit" as the headmistress referred to it, contained two to three students. A common room on each floor was used for studying and relaxing. Bedtime was ten o'clock. All lights were turned off then, and students were required to be in their beds. The dormitories were plain, with gray walls, thin carpet, and no televisions or radios permitted. The rooms were for relaxing and sleeping.

It was on the seventh floor that Dennis first met Lawrence Engels, Michael Scott, and Gregory Hollinsworth. Each lived on that floor. Gregory Hollinsworth would be Dennis's roommate.

They shared common bonds. Each was about six years from getting out of Westminster. Each thought of the school as a prison. Each had disappointed their family and had been sent to Westminster as punishment. They all were spirited non-conformists. Pole, Mouse, and Steam Pipe were like sticks of dynamite sitting harmlessly waiting for a match to ignite them. Dennis Morgan was the match. They were followers looking for a leader. He was a born leader, a born psychopath. They started with petty crimes — stealing food from the cafeteria, stealing cigarettes and small sundry items from the visitor gift shop and sundry store on the first floor. He was grooming his gang of four for bigger and better things. "They have to learn to walk before they run," he told himself. When Dennis thought they were ready to get a taste of blood on their hands, he devised a plan.

On the outskirts of the Westminster property, about two hundred yards from the center of campus was a chicken coop containing two-dozen chickens. The chicken coop was the idea of the headmistress. She enjoyed fresh eggs in the morning and saw the chicken coop as a way to satisfy her appetite as well as teach responsibility to her students.

Every week, a different group of four students was assigned the task of feeding and caring for the chickens, as well as harvesting the eggs. When it became the gang of four's turn to take care of the chickens, Dennis decided to implement his plan. The gang took four of the chickens into a storage shed on the other side of the property. The storage shed housed a tractor, several lawn mowers, hedge clippers, and other tools used to take care of the grounds. Dennis butchered the first chicken, slowly, sadistically, until all life left its body. Then he instructed the others to torture and dissect their chickens but to be slow and meticulous. He wanted to watch the chickens suffer. The idea was to prolong their suffering as long as possible before all life left their bodies. Dennis watched his prodigies as they did exactly what he told them to. He watched their eyes for signs of empathy toward their victims and watched their hands for any signs of apprehension. He watched their faces for any sign of revulsion. His prodigies had to be cold as ice. They could not feel empathy for their victims. Dennis had trained them well. They did as he asked, with no reservations and with no expression of weakness.

When the last chicken was dead, the gang took them to the dining hall. They laid the chickens out on a rack inside one of the ovens in the kitchen. Early the next morning, Erma Waters, an elderly woman with short, silver hair and thick, black-rimmed glasses that were several sizes too big for her face, pre-heated the oven to 375 degrees. She had made biscuits for the students and staff every morning for sixteen years. Her biscuits were light, fluffy, and made from an old family recipe that Erma refused to share with anyone. When her dough was ready, she placed them on two large cookie sheets and waited for the oven temperature to reach 375 degrees. When it did, she carried the first sheet of fresh biscuits over to the oven and opened the door. That's when she saw the four chickens, gutted, blood seeping down to the bottom of the oven, staring up at her. She screamed and fell to the floor, her sheet of biscuits following her, bouncing off the concrete floor.

Everyone at Westminster knew who was responsible for the dead chickens. The gang of four was sent to the headmistress's office. Waiting inside the office was Nancy Baczenas and three large men. They were part of the maintenance crew but also served as punishment enforcers when needed. She was in a somber mood. Those chickens were like pets to her. She had watched them grow up. Now, four of them were dead. She talked in a low but stern voice, staring directly into their faces as she talked.

"You boys have disappointed me. You have been given a great opportunity to turn your lives around at Westminster, an opportunity to make your parents proud, to make something out of your life, to grow and learn and develop into strong young men that will someday become leaders. But instead, you have embarrassed Westminster, you have embarrassed your fellow students, you have embarrassed me, and most importantly, you have embarrassed yourselves. For your own amusement, you destroyed four of God's creatures. You must be taught to respect life, respect me, and respect Westminster. For your punishment, each of you will spend one week in the basement—no classes, no interaction with other students, no recreation. You will be caged like the chickens you so callously murdered."

None of the boys had ever been to the basement before. Rumors of it had spread through the dormitory on occasion, but Dennis assumed stories about the basement were like urban legends, based on speculation and designed to maximize fear. He didn't believe any of the stories. The basement was cold, damp, and dark, the only light coming in from three small windows, maybe two-feet wide by two-feet deep positioned evenly along one wall. The floor was concrete, the walls made out of stone. There was one light in the hallway that remained on throughout the day and night. It illuminated the stairs leading down to the basement and a small section of the basement near those stairs. The rest of the basement remained dark after the sun went down. In the center of the basement was what only could be described as a cage. It was twelve-foot wide by twelve-foot deep, about the size of most bedrooms. Thick metal bars, approximately six inches apart, embedded into the floor and ceiling, surrounded all four sides of the cage.

Inside the cage were two bunk beds, a toilet, and a sink. A single thin white pillow and one brown blanket lay on each of the four beds. This would be the gang's home for seven days. The solitude and the isolation were designed to offer an opportunity for reflections on one's mistakes. Days were long, and nights were longer in that cage. The only sign of life outside the cage came three times a day when food was brought down to them. This type of punishment would have broken the will of most spirited boys, but not these boys. They had each other. Their bond grew stronger in that basement, as did their commitment for revenge.

The three windows were left open except during a storm. They were the only source of fresh air. At night, small creatures entered through the basement windows and cracks in the stone walls and concrete floor. Rats, mice, spiders, and an occasional snake would seek refuge in the basement. They wandered the concrete floor and stone walls of the basement, occasionally making their way into the cage that had become the boy's temporary home. The critters would stay awhile, then leave to seek refuge in another part of the basement. Sometimes they would crawl underneath the covers seeking a warm, comfortable spot to spend time.

One night, Pole woke up in the middle of the night to find a three-foot long black snake curled up under his blanket, next to his face. He screamed so loudly that faculty asleep on the fourth floor heard his cries through the ventilation system. Then he threw the snake clear across the room. Mouse and Steam Pipe laughed so hard they had tears streaming down their cheeks. Dennis was not amused. He was upset. He didn't expect any member of his gang to be afraid of something so trivial as a snake.

Dennis picked up the snake, still dazed from the force of hitting the wall, and carried the snake to where Pole was sitting.

"Hold its head tight," he barked at Pole.

Pole hesitated for a second until he saw the look on Dennis's face. He was pissed. He wasn't going to take "no" for an answer. Pole did as he was told.

"Now, take your other hand and hold the tail tight, keeping the body straight and rigid."

With the snake unable to move, Dennis pressed the tip of his fingernail on his index finger of his right hand directly into the skin of the snake just below its head. His fingernail was long and sharp after nearly a week without grooming it. Using the sharpest part of his fingernail, he penetrated the snake's skin. It squirmed and slithered, trying to get out of Pole's grasp.

"Damn it, hold it tight," Dennis yelled.

Pole tightened his grasp. Dennis dug deeper below the skin of the snake until blood began to surface. Then he slowly ripped the skin downward with his index finger. When a healthy part of the skin had been pulled down, he used his other fingers to pull the skin all the way down to the tail of the snake. Blood coated his fingers as he peeled the skin completely off. Sometime during the skinning, the snake stopped struggling.

When its skin was completely removed, and the snake had ceased suffering, Dennis looked directly into Pole's eyes. "Don't ever be afraid of anything. You have control. You are the hunter, not the hunted. Take this snake, put it under your pillow, and sleep with it. It will be a constant reminder that you can take life whenever you want."

After seven days and nights in the basement, Nancy Baczenas and the same three men that brought the boys to the basement paid them a visit. Pole, Mouse, and Steam Pipe were removed from the cage and allowed to go back to their dormitory. Dennis remained. He was the leader. His spirit would need to be broken in order to break the others' spirits. The headmistress explained the additional punishment to Dennis.

"I do not blame the others for what they have done. I blame you. Dennis, you have a powerful talent as a born leader. That talent could be put to good use. Your ability to motivate others could make such a positive difference in the lives of so many of the students here. Leadership is a virtue that is God-given. No one can learn it. People are either born leaders, or they're not. I would hope that you would work with me in the future to lead our students in a more positive way. It is your choice to make. Your years at Westminster can be productive. You might even enjoy them if you just learn to use your talents for the greater good. But, like I said, that is your choice. I will say that if you continue on your current destructive path, life at Westminster will become more challenging for you. Dennis, I am going to give you one more week down here to consider your future. Perhaps the solitude and simplicity of life in the basement will provide you the proper atmosphere to reflect on your future."

Nancy Baczenas didn't wait for a response from Dennis. She didn't expect one. She turned and walked away, going up the stairs and turning out the only light in the basement on her way. That light would remain out the entire week. The nights in the basement would be nearly completely dark, with the exception of the moonlight shining through the three small windows. Dennis's only company was the small critters that wandered in through the open windows and cracks in the wall and floor. Even the cafeteria workers that brought him three meals a day were instructed not to talk to him. They would open the cage, set down the tray of food on the concrete floor and walk away.

The food that Dennis didn't eat he would save and feed to the critters that paid him a visit in the evening. The solitude and quiet didn't bother him. In fact, he embraced it. It gave him time for reflection, but not the same reflection that Nancy Baczenas had hoped for. His reflection took a darker side. He planned revenge on the headmistress that had sent him and his gang to the basement. In a way, she had done him a favor, although he would never admit it. When he got out of the basement, he would be a legend among the other students. They would look up to him, they would respect him, they would be afraid of him because of what he endured during his time in the basement. But more than anything, he had time to think about the future, about the years after he got out of Westminster and about his plan for revenge against his mother for sending him to Westminster. Dennis had many reasons for hating his mother, but, most of all, he hated her for having what he did not, the Adler family wealth.

***

Dennis learned a valuable lesson from his time in the basement of Westminster. He learned not to get caught with his future crimes. The notoriety of his recent crime had served a purpose. It had established the gang of four as a force to be reckoned with. All the students knew them now. They either respected the gang, or they were afraid of them. Either way, they would not stand in their way. Whatever the gang wanted, they took. The only person that stood in their way was headmistress Nancy Baczenas and her enforcers. But she wouldn't stand in their way very long.

The massive storm that hit parts of nine states that fall was stronger and more powerful than predicted. It struck with hurricane force winds that downed power lines and disrupted electricity to almost every area in its path. Westminster went dark and lost all power about seven on a Thursday evening. Wind gusts up to eighty-miles-an-hour kept the students and staff inside, hunkered down in their rooms. Rain was pelting the building at almost a horizontal angle. Windows were bowing inward—several cracked, and three shattered. Leaks from a roof several years past needing repair trickled into several of the upper-level rooms, forcing a handful of students to seek refuge in the basement. Candles provided the only light that evening. Wind colliding with the century-old building and its four-foot-high glass windows echoed throughout the building, sounding like a whistle blasting in a tunnel.

Everyone stayed in their rooms, afraid to venture past their safe confines. Except for Nancy Baczenas—she wasn't afraid. She had been through countless storms over the years. "The worst of it is nearly over now," she told herself. "The rain and wind will weaken soon."

The headmistress needed to inspect the damage, check on the boys that had taken refuge in the basement, and make sure her staff was okay. She walked the fourth floor, checking on the occupants of every room and making a mental note of the damage and the repairs that would be needed. From there, she went to the third floor, walking down the same flight of steps she had traveled up and down for fifty-one years. She held a candlestick with a long, narrow white candle in her right hand. It provided her only visibility. The light from the candle swayed to the right and left with every movement she made. It provided just enough light to see a few feet in front of her. Fifteen steps down to the third floor. The stairs were steep and long, long enough to allow for the twelve-foot ceilings on each floor. Going down those steps wasn't the challenge. It was going back up them. She figured she had gone up and down those stairs over a million times during her time at Westminster. It had always been a good exercise, but lately, her aged body had begun to struggle with the daily grind of those stairs.

The third floor was completely quiet. No one resided on that floor. It was used for offices. Most of the doors were locked. One by one, Nancy took out her master key from her pocket, unlocked each door, and went inside to inspect for damage. There was one broken window, but no water damage. The leaks that fell from the roof onto the eighth floor had not penetrated the lower floors. Every office was locked and secured, except for one. At the end of the hall, the last office on the left, the door was open. It was the nurse's office. Beatrice Barker was the nurse. She was part-time, though, working only Tuesday, Thursday, and Saturday mornings. She had been in earlier that day but left around noon. All staff members were required to lock their office doors at the end of the day. Nurse Barker was aware of that rule.

Nancy moved slowly to the door and could hear a noise coming from inside. It sounded like a low-pitched cry. When she was within a foot of the door, she felt a cool breeze coming from the room. She lifted her candle directly in front of her and stepped into the room. A strong breeze took hold of her candle and blew the light out. She reached in her pocket for a match, and just as she pulled it out, she heard the cry and felt something hit her, causing her to lose her balance and fall to the floor.

It was a cat—she just saw its tail flashing by her and down the hall. The window in the office had shattered. Rain and wind were coming in. *The cat must have come in through the broken window,* she thought. She picked up the candle, relit it with a match, closed and locked the office door, and walked down the stairs to the second floor, which contained classrooms and conference rooms. In addition, there were art, library, and music rooms. As she had on the third and fourth floors, she checked every room, made sure the doors were locked and the room was secure and made notes of any damage.

The rain was beginning to slow and was no longer coming down at a horizontal angle. The wind was diminishing too. Two hours until daylight — the storm would be ending soon.

She descended the next fifteen stairs to the first floor. That floor contained the cafeteria, visitor gift shop, and a sundry store. In addition, it contained the grand entranceway and a welcome center. As she had on the other floors, she checked each room and each hallway. When she was finished, she moved toward the basement. Six staff members and eight students had taken refuge in the basement when the roof leaked rain into the eighth floor. Nancy Baczenas wanted to check on them before returning upstairs.

The hallway leading to the basement door was dark. The candle she was carrying had burned down to just a couple of inches — the wick had nearly disappeared. She raised the candle directly in front of her eyes with her right hand and opened the basement door with her left. The basement door was thick, old, and its hinges were rusty, so it squeaked loudly as it opened, so loudly that she didn't hear the person coming up behind her.

The headmistress felt the push, then felt herself losing balance. The candlestick slipped out of her hand and hit the stairs, shattering as it bounced on the hardwood steps. She struggled to regain her balance, steadying her right foot on the top step to gain control. Then she felt the second push, this one more forceful than the first. That push was enough to cause her to tumble, hitting her head against the railing, then the wood steps, and finally the basement's concrete floor. Somewhere between the fourth and tenth step, she snapped her neck.

CHAPTER 13
A PLAN WITH CONSEQUENCES

The death of Nancy Baczenas was ruled an accident. She tumbled down the stairs in the dark. The staff members and students in the basement at the time of the accident did not see or hear anything out of the ordinary. They heard a scream, followed by the sound of her body hitting and rolling down the stairs. That was it. There was no reason to suspect foul play. The gang of four would never talk about the accident. Her death was a tragedy for Westminster, but it also eliminated the last roadblock that stood in the way of the gang of four. No one, after the headmistress's death, stood up to the gang of four. Their crimes for the next five years went unchecked within the walls of Westminster. Dennis had given his followers a taste of killing. Like him, they enjoyed it. He was their leader. He had complete control of them. Even as their time at Westminster ended, they knew they would come together again. Their bond was strong, their dependence on Dennis Morgan even stronger.

So, when he summoned them to the Adler mansion a few years later, no one hesitated. They did exactly as he told them, putting their lives on hold to do as their leader requested. Now, one of them was dead. Mouse had been killed in his struggle with Connor at the bottom of the hidden stairway. Pole discovered his body soon after he discovered the rear stairs leading to the fourth floor. Dennis had sent him in the basement to find Mouse.

He told him about the hidden stairway and where to find it. But he wasn't to go up those stairs, not yet anyway. His instructions were that the gang was to complete all of their tasks before going up to the fourth floor. Pole was only in that area of the basement to look for Mouse, who was supposed to join the rest of the gang on the first floor after retrieving the money and receipts from the safe. When he didn't show, Pole was sent down to find him. The accounting office was a mess. The safe was open, the money gone. He walked nearly every inch of the basement looking for Mouse before he discovered the blood on the floor between racks of seasonal items. He saw the nail that had been used as a weapon, coated in blood and lying on the concrete floor just a few feet from the bloodstain. Pole knew at that point that something had gone terribly wrong with Dennis's plan, and he had a sick feeling that he wouldn't find Mouse alive.

When he saw his friend lying underneath the stairwell, covered in blood and with a long, narrow sewing knife sticking out of his chest, his first thoughts were not sadness, or fear, or anger. They were of greed. There would be one less person to split the money with. Ice ran through Pole's veins. He was incapable of feeling empathy for anyone but himself. He had known Mouse for over ten years, yet he was unable to shed a tear or feel any remorse for his murder. Dennis had trained him well.

He returned to the first floor to report what he'd found. Dennis's only comment was, "Did you find the black duffle bag?"

"No," he responded.

Dennis didn't express concern. He was confident that the black duffle bag was now on the fourth floor. They would retrieve it soon. Now his biggest concern was to complete loading up the truck sitting at the dock on the first floor. He had been given a list of the items to load in the truck by Bill Collins. Now that Old Man Collins was dead, Dennis had a new boss. But his instructions hadn't changed. He had loaded all the items on the list except for a cherry red jewelry box. It was the last item on the list and contained special instructions not to open the box and to place it on the passenger's seat in the cab of the truck. The box had been hidden by Bill Collins. It was of particular importance to him. Dennis thought he would have hidden the box in the security office. Mouse opened every drawer, looked in every area of that office, but did not find it. At least, Dennis assumed that he didn't find it. Mouse was given specific instructions that if he found the jewelry box, he was to bring it to Dennis immediately.

The possibility did cross Dennis's mind that perhaps Mouse found the jewelry box and placed it inside the black duffle bag instead of bringing it to him. They had searched every inch of the first and second floors. Dennis was confident that the jewelry box was not on either of those floors. That meant it had to be in the basement or on the fourth floor.

Dennis had one regret about killing Bill Collins. That regret was that he didn't get him to reveal the hiding place of that red jewelry box before he killed him. If he had, Dennis's mission at Adler that night would be completed, and he would be gone. But now time was running out. Only ninety minutes until daylight. Dennis would need to hurry.

He assigned Pole half of the basement area to search for the box. He assigned Steam Pipe the other half. Dennis would search the offices. They were instructed to bring the box directly to Dennis if they found it. If no one found the box within thirty minutes, they were to meet at the bottom of the rear staircase. Dennis searched every inch of all three offices. He even searched the body of Bill Collins, hoping to find some clue to where the jewelry box was hidden. There was nothing. Both Pole and Steam Pipe came up empty too. *The box must be on the fourth floor*, Dennis thought.

So, thirty minutes after they began the search, the three men met at the bottom of the rear staircase. There was only one other place to search, the fourth floor. It was always Dennis's plan to finish on the fourth floor. Now, with only an hour of darkness remaining, he needed to expedite his plan.

***

The old wooden stairs creaked as the three men began to ascend them. Connor could hear them as they approached. So could David Morgan. "You, better hide," he told Connor. "They will kill you if they find you."

"What about you?" Connor asked.

"I will know soon if I need to hide. Just tell the ghosts to let me in if I open the door to the showroom."

"I will," Connor said, knowing it would not do any good. The ghosts would not let David enter that room. They had told Connor that already. "What about the black duffle bag? Do you want me to take it into the showroom?"

"No. If all goes as planned, I will need that duffle bag. And if things don't go as planned, I will bring it with me into the other room."

Connor nodded his head. That was not the answer he wanted to hear, but he wasn't about to argue with a crazy man holding a gun. He turned to the door, turned the doorknob to the right, and slowly opened the door.

The showroom was completely dark. The ghosts were not there. The room was completely bare, with no good places to hide. Where were the ghosts? Where was his grandfather? Had he made a mistake by counting on what his grandfather had said to him? After all, he wasn't actually talking to his grandfather. He was talking to a ghost that looked like his grandfather. Connor didn't believe in ghosts. Maybe the bump on his head that he received from David Morgan did damage to his brain. Maybe he just thought he saw ghosts. His grandfather had died years earlier. It didn't make sense that he would appear that night. How stupid could he be? Because he listened to what those figments of his imagination said, he was now trapped on the fourth floor with killers coming up the stairs and with no place to hide.

Connor was in trouble and couldn't go back down the

stairs. The boy was trapped on the fourth floor. The strangers would be coming to find him soon. There was one exit, but that would mean going through the vent in the bedroom, which would mean he would need to go to the other side of the wall, to the hidden room. That was where the other ghosts were, the bad ghosts, according to David. If he could get by them, he could reach the stairs leading to the roof. From there, he could exit down the fire escape.

David was waiting on the other side of the door. He had a gun and would likely put up resistance if Connor tried to leave that way. Trying to escape that way would be dangerous. If David didn't stop him, the ghosts surely would. But staying in a room with no good hiding place was dangerous too. Escaping through that vent wasn't a good option, but it was an option. Whatever decision Connor made would need to be done soon. The footsteps on the stairs were getting louder. The strangers would be on the fourth floor soon.

Connor decided on his best option. There was no way out of the showroom. With no place to hide, the strangers would easily find him. The boy needed to get to the vent in the other room. He moved to the door and slowly, quietly, carefully opened it just enough to get a view of the back room, hoping to spot the old man. If his back was turned and if he was far enough away from the bedroom, perhaps Connor could get to the vent without being noticed. Then he could unscrew the vent screen and wait until the strangers met David at the top of the stairs. When that happened, hopefully, the distraction would be enough for Connor to escape through the vent without being heard. He would worry about the ghosts when he got to the other side.

With the door opened only a few inches, Connor's line of sight was narrow. The old man was not in his sight. He opened the door a little more carefully so as not to be heard. The sound of footsteps climbing the back stairway was louder now. The gait of those steps had slowed, but the sound of their feet landing on the steps was more pronounced. They were tiring, Connor reasoned. There were exactly sixty steps from the basement to the fourth floor, each one twelve inches higher than the one before it. Even an athlete like Connor got a little winded climbing those stairs.

Even with the door opened nearly a foot and Connor's line of sight increased dramatically, he could not see or hear David. Maybe he was already in the stairway, Connor thought. From the sounds of the footsteps, the strangers were very close, most likely no more than a floor away. He needed to move now. So, Connor opened the door all the way and glanced around the room for any sign of the crazed old man. When he didn't see him, Connor moved softly toward the bedroom on the right side of the back room. The room was completely dark. David had turned out the light that was in his bedroom. There were no other lights. *Is David hiding from the strangers or waiting for them?* Connor asked himself.

The darkness was a mixed blessing. It hid him from the sight of others, but it also made it difficult to find his way. With the room completely dark, Connor had to feel his way toward the bedroom. He knew about where it was, but there were many obstacles in his way. Unless he collided with something that made a noise that could be heard, it would be nearly impossible to see him in the dark. Except for that damn shirt he was wearing. The bright blue and red colors of the University of Kansas stood out like the glow from a flashlight. Connor couldn't see his hand in front of his face, but he sure as hell could see that shirt, even in total darkness.

Six steps, seven steps, eight steps—every step got him a little closer to the vent. Just inside the bedroom door, he saw a narrow bit of light coming from the rear of the storeroom. Someone was opening the door. The light was beaming from a flashlight moving up the stairs. Connor moved quickly to the vent—time was running out. He pulled out a penny from his pocket and used it to loosen the screws that were holding the vent screen in place. One screw, two screws, three screws — the light from the flashlight was getting brighter. The door to the stairs was all the way open now. They were no more than fifty feet away from him. His hands were shaking, his body was quivering. One screw left, and the vent screw could be removed. Nervous perspiration from his forehead was rolling down his cheeks and his arm. The wetness had made its way to his hand, making it difficult to maneuver the penny into the last screw. He steadied his right hand by holding his wrist still with his left hand. Connor had never been this afraid in his entire life. He could hear the voices of the strangers and could hear David Morgan's voice. The old man must have been waiting for them at the top of the stairs.

It was time to move through that vent. David was talking to the strangers. His voice would distract them from hearing Connor move through the vent. With his right hand steadied, Connor located the groove in the head of the screw and inserted the penny. He turned the penny counterclockwise once, then twice. The screw was loosening. He steadied his hand one more time to make one long, final turn to remove the screw. His hand was completely damp with perspiration. The moisture had slid to the tip of his index finger and onto the surface of the penny. As he began to turn the penny one last time, his hand slipped. The penny hit the side of the groove and fell to the floor. It bounced once and then rolled out of sight.

Connor dropped his head in disbelief. Then he heard it. One loud pop. A scream. Then a second loud pop. Connor had heard that sound before when he watched Bill Collins get murdered. It was the sound of a gun.

***

David looked down at the two bodies lying less than twenty feet from where he was standing at the top of the stairs. The body farthest away from him fell face-first onto the stairs, then slid down another few feet, resting halfway been the third and fourth floors. The second body, the one closest to him, fell backwards and landed on the step just below David Morgan's feet. His body fell at an angle to his right, resting against the brick wall of the building. Both men were killed instantly.

The look of fear on David's face was replaced with a smile. "Glad to see you are still alive, son," he said to Dennis.

"There was never a doubt, Dad. Everything went exactly as planned."

Pole and Steam Pipe never saw the betrayal coming. They had been loyal to Dennis right up until the end and had no idea that his plan included their death.

Father and son Morgan walked down the steps and back into the basement. The two of them walked into the security office to the closet in the back of the room. They opened the door and lifted the lifeless body of Bill Collins. His body was cold and had started to stiffen. They carried him to the back stairway, then dragged him slowly up the stairs, Dennis pulling him by the right arm and David pulling him by his left arm. Slowly they ascended the stairs until they got a few feet away from Steam Pipe.

They laid the dead security guard on the landing on the third floor. Dennis wiped the handle of the gun he had just used to kill his two friends, then reached for Bill Collins's right hand. It was closed. Rigor mortis had begun to set in. The hand was cold and stiff, locked in a clenched position. Dennis leveraged his index finger just underneath Bill Collins's pinky finger and pulled it open, and used the same technique to open the next two fingers. When he reached the index finger, it was locked in place. He used two fingers, wedging them just underneath the knuckle of Bill Collin's finger. When they were wedged far enough underneath, Dennis pulled. It did not budge. Again he tried, this time using more force, and something gave way. He fell backwards, landing on his back three steps below. Laying on his chest was the index finger of Bill Collins. It had snapped off.

Dennis used the finger to leave a print on the handle of the gun. Then he placed the finger and the gun next to the security guard's body. Out of his other pocket, Dennis pulled the gun that he had used to kill Bill earlier that evening. He placed that gun in the right hand of Pole.

Then Dennis turned his attention to the fourth floor. "Is he up there, Dad?"

"Yes."

"Do you know where he is hiding?"

"Yes"

"Do you have the black duffle bag?"

"Yes, I took it from him and hid it in a safe place."

"Let's go get it and take care of the boy."

***

Connor heard the conversation. The vent carried the voices from the stairway directly into the bedroom on the fourth floor. Just after hearing the gunshots, he removed the last screw holding the vent screen in place. Then he crawled under the bed and grabbed the black duffle bag that David Morgan had taken from him. The duffle bag was important to the strangers. They were coming for it. Connor needed to hide it. That bag could buy him more time. He grabbed it and carried it with him into the vent, shutting the vent screen behind him. Then he sat inside the vent and waited. From there, he could hear sounds coming from the other end of the vent. His body trembled with fear of what might be waiting for him on the other side of the wall. He'd heard the gunshots but had no idea who had been shot. Maybe he would be safe after all. Maybe he would not need to escape through the vent. The bad ghosts were on the other side. He could hear them stirring. It might be more dangerous for him to cross over to the other side than it was for him to stay put, so he decided to wait and listen. That seemed to be his best option.

Something, someone was on the other side of the wall. He had a good view of the bedroom through the other side of the vent screen. If the strangers entered the bedroom, he would see them and have time to escape through the vent to the other side of the wall. But he also knew that once he had entered that vent, there would only be one option to escape if the strangers came after him. If that happened, he would have to face them. The voices he heard at the other end of the vent were louder now. It sounded like people talking, carrying on a conversation that was just far enough away to be heard, but not clearly. He could not make out their words. If he moved inside the vent, the ghosts, if that's what they were, would hear his movement echoing through the aluminum walls of the vent. They would know where he was, and they would be waiting for him when he crossed through to the other side.

When he heard the conversation between David and his son, he knew that David had betrayed him. He had told his son about Connor. It occurred to Connor that David knew that his son planned to kill the other strangers. His plea to Connor to convince the ghosts to let him into the showroom was a contingency plan. If something went wrong and Dennis was killed, he would need to escape.

Connor took a deep breath and prepared to move inside the vent. They would enter the bedroom any time now, and he would need to move quickly. That's when he saw the narrow beam of light shooting through the storage room and catching the corner of his eye. He stopped and turned to look. The light was coming from the showroom. There was noise too — laughter, singing, people. Dennis and David heard them too. Connor thought about getting out of the vent and running to the door. The ghosts in the showroom would protect him. His grandfather had told him so. But the father and son were right outside the door. They would grab him before he was able to get to the showroom. Connor decided to wait in the vent.

***

Dennis and David moved through the storeroom to the door leading into the showroom. They heard the people on the other side. They saw the light coming from underneath the door.

"Where is the boy?" Dennis asked his father.

"I think he is inside that room," his father said.

Dennis tried to open the door. The doorknob wouldn't turn, locked from the other side. David was just behind him. He grabbed the gun out of his father's hands, pointed it at the doorknob, and fired, once, twice, three times, until the knob and lock shattered and the force of the third bullet pushed the door open.

Dennis stood at the open door, frozen in place and unable to believe his eyes. His father stood a few steps behind him. "I told you about this room. I told you what I had seen before."

Dennis had heard his mother talk about this room many times before. She talked fondly of the glory days of Adler when this room was the centerpiece of the store. Only the wealthiest and most influential of its clientele were invited to this room. Now he saw men drinking whiskey, smoking cigars, and conducting business. Their wives sipped wine, socialized, and watched the runway models showcase the latest in fashions. Everything he saw today was exactly how his mother had described it when the fourth floor was in its prime over twenty years ago. He closed his eyes, thinking that his mind was playing tricks on him and that when he opened them again, everything would be gone. But it wasn't. The clothes the people were wearing came from a time long ago. The furniture, the fixtures, the fine oak bar, and the two massive fireplaces looked polished and brand new. People in the room conducted themselves as if he wasn't there. He was witnessing a night on the Adler fourth floor that, as impossible as it appeared, looked like it was happening many years before.

That's when he saw the calendar hanging on a wall just behind the oak bar. Saturday, December 7, 1947. Dennis nudged his father to look at the date on the calendar. When he read it, David Morgan nearly fell to the floor. He remembered that date. It had been etched in his memory for twenty-six-years. Saturday, December 7, 1947, was the date that he murdered Thomas Adler.

CHAPTER 14
CORRECTING FATE

David Morgan pulled his son back into the storage room and shut the door.

"What the hell are you doing?" Dennis shouted at his father.

"We can't go in there. I know what is going on. They have come for me."

David Morgan was visibly shaken. He was white as a sheet. His eyes were wide open, and he was staring into blank space. His hands were trembling.

"Listen, Dad. I don't know what we saw in the other room. I don't know if it was our imagination. But I do know that whatever we think we saw was not real. Whatever is on the other side of that door cannot hurt us. We need to go back. We need to take care of the boy. He is the only witness left."

Dennis reached for his father's arm. David Morgan ran. He ran into the bedroom and shut and locked the door. Dennis ran after him. When he got to the locked door, he raised his foot and kicked the area just underneath the doorknob with all his force. The door flew open. He found his father curled up on the bed in a fetal position. He had pulled the covers around him and had wrapped his arms around the back of his head, forcing his face to be buried in the bedsheets. His father was shaking and crying. What the old man had seen in the showroom of the fourth floor was enough to send his mind into a downward spiral of which there was no pulling out of. Fear had paralyzed him. It was at that moment that Dennis was more afraid than he had ever been. The thin line his father had been walking between sanity and insanity had eroded into complete darkness. There was no reasoning with him now. It was up to Dennis to finish what he had started.

"The boy was trapped in the showroom. He could not go anywhere," he said to himself.

Dennis would wait to go into the showroom again until he had searched the back room. He needed to find the last item on his list, the red jewelry box. It had to be on the fourth floor. The gang had searched every inch of the other floors.

Dennis began his search near the stairway leading downstairs. He would save searching the bedroom for last to give his father some time to collect himself. With no light other than his flashlight, the search would be challenging. Time was running out—less than an hour until daylight. He used the flashlight to guide him through every square inch of the back room. The red jewelry box, as described on his list, was twelve inches long by nine inches deep. It was bright red in color with gold-plated edges. It was large enough and colorful enough that it should be easy to find, Dennis thought.

When he found the opening in the floor that revealed a secret hiding spot just large enough to hide an item the size of the jewelry box, he thought he had found its hiding place. But the area was empty. Maybe it was there at one time, and someone removed it. Maybe his father removed it. When he exhausted his search in the back room, he moved to the bedroom. There was no time to waste. If the jewelry box was in the bedroom, his father put it there, Dennis reasoned. Thirty minutes remaining until daylight.

He flipped on the light to the bedroom. His father was still lying on the bed, curled up, face covered and mumbling to himself. Dennis grabbed him, pulled him up, and slapped him in the face. "Where the hell is the jewelry box, and where the hell is the duffle bag?" Dennis wasn't in the mood, nor did he have time to coddle his father. He needed to bring him back to reality as quickly as possible. A second smack to the face, then a third, before finally, a bit of sanity returned to his father's eyes.

"I've never seen a red jewelry box," he said, holding his right hand up to his reddened face.

"What about the duffle bag?"

"It's under the bed."

Dennis bent down and looked under the bed. It wasn't there. Dennis lifted the gun to his father's head. "I'm only going to ask you one more time. Where the hell is the duffle bag?"

"It was under the bed. I swear. The kid must have taken it. It has to be in the other room with him."

"Listen, old man. We are going into the other room. We are going to take care of the boy. We are going to find that duffle bag and the red jewelry box, and then we're going to get the hell out of here before the sun comes up. Do you hear me?"

"Yes," his father said. For the first time in his life, David was afraid of his son. He was more afraid of him than he was of facing what was on the other side of the door.

They left the room and walked toward the door. Dennis followed behind his father, making sure that he couldn't run. There was something different about the light beaming from the bottom of the door. It was not as bright. It was softer, with a little glow to it.

"Open the door," he said to his father, whose hand was trembling.

David did as he was told. The doorknob and lock had shattered when his son shot it earlier. The soft glow of light was pouring in through the hole, but something was different about this light—it was bouncing as it streaked through the hole. It was not just white as the reflections from the light had been the last time they got to the door. There was no laughter, no music, no distinguishable conversation going on behind the door. The glow of light took on an orange, yellow, and red color. Colors were intertwined together as they jumped through the hole in the door. He heard a cracking sound coming from the distance, and then he smelled a hint of smoke. The room was on fire, he thought. David tried to back up. Then he felt the barrel of the gun in his back.

"Open the damn door," his son demanded.

David had no choice. He did as he was told. He put his fingers through the hole in the door and pulled it open.

The room was dark, quiet. Then he saw the source of the colors he had been jetting through the hole in the door. It was the fireplace on the far left side of the room. Logs in the fireplace were burning, their flames strong, shooting up the flue and sending the glow of light and smell of smoke into the room. There were no other lights on in the room. The room appeared to be exactly as he had seen it a short time earlier. The furniture and the grand oak bar were there. The large, crystal chandeliers hung from the tall ceiling. There were two massive fireplaces, one on each side of the room. Everything looked the same, except the people were gone. He turned to look in the bar area. The calendar was still there, but it showed a different date—December 11, 1963. Everything looked so familiar.

Suddenly, everything came into focus for David Morgan. A warm feeling trickled through his body. A feeling of complete calm came over him. He was no longer afraid. He was no longer walking a thin line between sanity and insanity. It had been a long, painful journey for him. But now he was going home.

The old man moved forward into the room. His son followed. As he got closer to the sounds he was hearing, he could see the images of two people lying naked on the couch next to the fireplace. David stood just a few feet away from them. They were in a passionate embrace. Dennis moved to the side of his father and stared down at the two lovers.

"Stand up," Dennis shouted to them.

They ignored him as if they hadn't heard his demand.

"Stand up, damn it," he screamed with a more forceful tone.

They ignored him again.

Dennis raised his gun and pointed it directly at the head of the man, who was now on top of the woman. Her legs were spread, her legs lifted, and her feet curled around the shoulders of her lover. They did not interrupt their lovemaking.

"This is your last warning. Get up, or I'm going to put a bullet in your heads!"

The couple showed no sign of stopping. They didn't acknowledge his presence. They acted as if they hadn't heard a word he had said.

Dennis fired the gun directly into the back of the man's head, once, twice, and finally, a third shot. The barrel of the gun was no more than a few inches from the man's head. The man did not move—no blood shot from his head. There was no indication that the man even heard the gunshot.

"That's impossible," Dennis said out loud. In a final fit of anger, the boy brought the gun barrel toward his body, and with all his force, he slammed it down on the head of the man on the couch, aiming directly for his head. He expected to feel the contact when the gun's barrel collided with the man's head, but instead, the gun continued through the two lovers and collided with the cushions on the couch. His body lost balance when it didn't collide with the man's head, and Dennis fell onto the sofa and then rolled off onto the wood floor.

His eyes caught sight of his father just before his head collided with the floor. David Morgan was smiling. He was staring at the sofa, and he was smiling. His face was cold and emotionless except for that shitty, strange smile.

The blow of his head hitting the hardwood floor dazed Dennis a little. He laid there on his back for a few seconds, just staring at the ceiling, trying not to pass out. That's when he heard the noise. It sounded like something coming up through the walls on the other side of the room. He reached for his gun, which had fallen on the floor with him and landed just a few feet away. Dennis grabbed it. It was out of bullets. *Damn it*, he thought. He'd used the last bullet shooting at the couple on the couch. He slammed the gun down on the floor and lifted himself up.

The lovers were still on the couch, in the midst of passion. The man was still on top of the woman. He had quickened the movement of his body. His breathing was heavy. Her excitement was increasing. They were no longer quiet.

Dennis focused his eyes on the area of the wall where he heard the noise. One beep, then the sound of a motor pulling something. Two beeps. The sound of the motor continued. Three beeps. The motor sound stopped. Then he saw it. Where the blank wall had been, in the area the noise was coming from, there now was the outside of an elevator. It had appeared the second the third beep was heard. Above the elevator door was a light with the numbers 1, 2, 3, and 4 on it. The number four was brighter than the others. The door opened, and out stepped two men. One was an old man, well-dressed in a black, pin-striped suit with a white handkerchief in his suit pocket and a black tie. Dennis didn't recognize him. But the second man he knew. He had killed him just a few hours earlier. That man was Bill Collins. He was younger, thinner, he had more hair, but it was Bill Collins. Dennis was certain.

The two men walked off the elevator together and walked slowly toward the couch, next to the fireplace, where the two lovers were in the heat of passion. Bill Collins slowed as he approached the lovers, letting the older gentleman walk ahead. Just as the old man reached the edge of the sofa, the two lovers reached their final climax together. Their cries of ecstasy drowned out the tears and soft cries from the old man. He watched, shaken and a broken man, as the stranger lifted off his wife.

The back of the man on the couch was turned to the old man when he heard the first gunshot. It whizzed by his left ear, embedding itself in the back of the sofa. His lover screamed. He ran. The second bullet hit him squarely in the back, shattering his spine. He fell to the floor, unable to move. He heard his lover scream one more time before the sound of the next bullet silenced her forever. Then he heard one more shot. Laying on the floor, out of the corner of his eye, he saw the old man fall to the floor. Then he watched, unable to move, as Bill Collins, smoke still coming out of the barrel of his gun, walked slowly toward him. When he was just inches away, Bill pointed the gun directly at David Morgan's heart and pulled the trigger.

Dennis stood, stone-faced and in disbelief of what he had just seen. What he had just witnessed had to be his mind playing tricks on him. Maybe he was going crazy. Maybe he was already crazy. Nothing he had just witnessed could be real. He turned to where his father had been standing, wondering if he saw the same thing. He wasn't there. Instead, his father was lying on the ground where Bill Collins had shot him. He watched as his father's body slowly rose and then disappeared. David Morgan's soul was no longer lost. Dennis's father had gone home.

Dennis was left standing by himself. In an instant, everyone and everything in that room was gone. The elevator that had brought the two men up to the fourth floor was gone. The fireplace was there, but the logs and fire were not. There were no bodies, no bloodstains, and no indication that what he had just witnessed ever took place. Dennis was standing in complete darkness. A coldness suddenly came over the room where warmth from the fireplace had been. He moved quickly toward the back room. Whatever he had seen in the showroom could not be real. His mind had to be playing tricks on him. He needed to get out of that room. His father had disappeared. The boy was not in that showroom. They had to be in the other room.

That was the only explanation. His father had been afraid of the showroom. When Dennis was watching the scene playing out in front of him, his father must have run into the other room. That was the only thing that made sense.

The other room was dark, quiet. There was no sign of his father or the boy. They had to be there, he told himself. It was the only place they could be.

Then, he heard the voices. It sounded like men talking in the distance. They grew louder as he neared the bedroom. He couldn't make out what they were saying. There was an echo to the sound he heard as if they were talking in a tunnel. The voices sounded angry. He moved closer to the sounds, closer to the vent.

***

Connor watched as he approached, ready to move to the other side of the wall. But something was holding him back. Maybe it was the angry voices coming from the other side. Or maybe it was the voice in his head that told him that he would be safe if he just stayed where he was. The voice in his head was his grandfather talking to him. He was dead. It was crazy that Connor would listen to a voice from someone that had died many years earlier. But he did. When he was alive, his grandfather was always there for him. Then, there was the time Connor was trapped in the bedroom with the fire raging in the other room. He nearly died that day. But his grandfather came to him and saved his life. He was dead then, too. There was something calming in his grandfather's voice. Connor listened to the voice in his head and stayed where he was even as Dennis Morgan pulled the vent screen off and saw him just a few feet away.

The crazed youth reached for Connor's legs. Connor kicked and tried to pull away, but Dennis's grip was strong. He began pulling him out of the vent. Connor kicked one last time, using all his strength, and managed to break free of Dennis's grasp. Connor threw the duffle bag as far as he could through the vent. It fell onto the floor on the other side of the wall. Then

Dennis grabbed hold of both his legs and pulled him out of the vent. The anger in his eyes told Connor that he wanted to kill him. Dennis lifted him up and flung his body across the room.

Connor was dazed. His head had hit the floor hard. He thought he was going to pass out and expected Dennis to jump on top of him. He thought he was going to die. But instead, he saw him climb into the vent. Getting that duffle bag was his top priority.

Killing Connor could wait. Dennis crawled quickly into the area where the bad ghosts lived. The duffle bag was only a few feet away.

Connor had only a few seconds to react before Dennis came back for him. He lifted his body off the floor and ran toward the showroom door. For a moment, he considered running toward the hidden stairway leading back to the basement, but something told him to go into the showroom. It was his grandfather talking to him again. As he got past the bedroom door, a light began to beam through the hole in the showroom door. He could hear voices, music, and laughter coming from the other room.

***

Dennis made his way to the other side of the vent, just five feet from the duffle bag lying on the floor in the secret room. He stepped out of the vent, moved three feet inside the room, and reached for the duffle bag. That's when he felt the pain in his back. Out of the corner of his right eye, he saw the figure standing over him holding a knife, the blade coated in blood. Dennis had been stabbed. He pulled the gun out of his pocket and pointed it at the man. When the man lunged at him one more time with the knife, Dennis pulled the trigger, but nothing happened. The gun was out of bullets. He closed his eyes, waiting for the final pain of the knife blade that would likely end his life. But instead, he heard the sound of the knife bouncing off the concrete floor. He opened his eyes. The figure that was wielding the knife vanished. *Was it my imagination?* he wondered. But the pain in his back wasn't his imagination. He moved his left hand to the spot of his pain. When he moved his hand back to take a look, the palm of his hand was smeared in blood.

He reached for the duffle bag and picked it up with his left hand while he held his gun with his right hand. Just as he lifted the duffle bag, he saw two men standing on the other side of the room, both holding knives. They were looking directly at him. One of the men, heavyset, with black hair and a good six inches taller than the other man, spoke to him.

"It's time to go home," he said. Then, both men lunged toward him.

Dennis climbed quickly into the vent and crawled as fast as possible toward the other side. He felt a hand grab his foot. He kicked it and felt the hand slip off his foot. The men did not follow him into the vent. When he got out on the bedroom side of the vent, he ran out the room and to the door leading into the showroom. He had the bag. Now he just needed to take care of the boy and find the red jewelry box. Maybe it was in the duffle bag. When he was safely on the other side, he would open it and check.

When he reached the door to the showroom, he turned to look behind. The men that he had seen in the hidden room had not followed him. With that danger behind him, he turned back to the door and saw the light beaming out of the hole in the door. On the other side of the door, people were talking, laughing, carrying on conversations. He heard the music.

Just as he started to take his first steps back to the other room, a fog began to come out of both fireplaces. It was light at first, then thickened. As the fog became dense, it began to consume every part of the room. He hesitated before opening the door. Dennis thought about exiting down the rear stairs, but then he thought about the people that had sent him to Adler that night. They were not the sort of people that you wanted to betray. They had given him a list of what they wanted. He had collected everything except that red jewelry box. They gave him specific instructions to get that jewelry box. They also had given specific instructions not to leave any witnesses. The people that sent him there would not be happy. Then, there was his father. His father had disappeared. He needed to find him if he was still alive. And, if he was still alive, he needed to kill him, too.

So he entered the showroom to finish what he had started. The room came alive again, exactly as it had been earlier in the evening. The room was bright. It was crowded with people. Music was playing from a piano in the far corner of the room. A bartender was busy pouring drinks and talking to customers. Women were crowded around the fireplace, sitting on the furniture that was a murder scene just minutes earlier. Men were crowded around the other fireplace, sipping brandy and smoking cigars. The room was full of laughter and conversation.

On the other side of the room was the elevator, and standing next to it was the boy, talking to an older, distinguished-looking man with wavy, salt and pepper hair. The older man was holding an open red jewelry box. Dennis Morgan watched as the boy put his hand in the box and pulled out a large, gold key.

That was the jewelry box on the list of items Dennis had been given to load in the truck. Time was running out. The sun would start rising over the horizon any time now. Dennis began moving quickly toward the boy. He needed to get that jewelry box. He needed to kill the boy.

Connor saw him coming out of the corner of his eye. He grabbed the key and quickly moved to the elevator. The door opened, and he entered. He put the key inside a keyhole just inside the elevator, turned the key clockwise, and the door began to close. Just then, Dennis Morgan reached the elevator door, putting his right hand inside it to stop its progress. The door stopped closing. Just as Dennis was about to grab Connor, a strong gust of wind lifted him backwards and tossed him on the floor. As he laid on the floor, he watched as the door closed, and

Connor disappeared.

He watched as the elevator descended to the third floor. Then, the elevator door disappeared, and nothing but a bare wall replaced it. He got to his feet and glanced around the room. The people had stopped what they were doing. The music had stopped. Everyone was staring at him. The man that the boy had been talking to, the man with salt and pepper hair, reached his hand out to Dennis. "It's time to go home," he said. "Let me show you the way."

Dennis moved away from him. He must be going crazy. None of this could be real. From behind him, a fog began to enter the room from the fireplace, and it moved quickly into the room, covering every inch of it within just a few seconds. The fog became too dense for Dennis to see anything. Then, as quickly as it had appeared, the fog disappeared. When he could see again, the people were gone, and the room was empty. The furniture, the chandeliers, the bar, the piano, everything was gone. The room was bare, cold, and looked like it had been neglected for many years.

CHAPTER 15
THE FIRE

When the door closed on the elevator, Connor pressed the button to the first floor. He hoped to get off the elevator and escape through the front door, or if it was locked, through the door by the shipping dock, the same door that the strangers had entered several hours earlier. But when the elevator reached the third floor, it stopped, and the door opened. Connor waited inside the elevator, pressing the first-floor button over and over again. The elevator did not move. The door remained open. With reluctance, he removed the key from the elevator, put it in his pocket, and exited the elevator. The door to the elevator closed behind him. Then, like magic, the elevator completely disappeared. A solid white wall replaced it. It was as if the elevator had never existed.

Everything was completely dark on the third floor except a little light coming through the windows on the east side of the floor, where the morning sun was beginning to peek over the horizon. Then he saw it: nothing, absolutely nothing. The showroom floor was completely bare. Even the display cases were gone. The floor was completely devoid of its usual merchandise and display cases. Cash registers, mannequins, carpeting, advertisements, and lighting were all gone. Paint was peeling from the walls. Something else, too — the floor was filthy, dust and dirt everywhere. There were even cobwebs hanging from the walls and ceiling. What he saw was impossible. Connor had been on this floor just a few hours earlier. He had swept and waxed it. Everything looked normal then. Sometime, during the middle of the night, everything had disappeared. Was his mind playing tricks on him? He had, after all, seen ghosts, even talked to them. Nothing in Adler was the way he remembered.

***

Dennis Morgan barely escaped the ghosts. His knife wound was not serious, but it hurt like hell. He needed to get the wound tended to. But first, he needed to get that gold key, and he needed to take care of the boy. The people that sent him to Adler that night would be waiting on the first floor. The plan called for them to meet him there just before sunrise. He was late. They would be angry. And, when they found out the boy was still alive and he was in possession of the gold key, they would blame him. These were not the type of people you wanted to disappoint. Dennis would need to convince them that he could take care of the boy and get the gold key if they would just allow him a little more time.

Dennis ran to the hidden staircase. He needed to beat the boy to the first floor. He took six steps down the stairs and suddenly stopped. Where were the bodies of his two friends? They were gone. The bodies were not where he had left them. They were nowhere around. Bill Collins's body was gone too. But there was no time to worry about them. Dennis knew they were dead. That was the only thing he needed to be concerned about. Now he needed to take care of the boy.

He moved quickly down the hidden stairway, past the third floor, past the second floor, past the first floor. He opened the door leading into the basement and stopped. Everything was gone. The sewing room was no longer there. The shelves containing seasonal items were gone. The mannequins, the storage boxes, everything in the basement had disappeared. Was he too late? The sun was coming up. They'd told him he needed to be done by sunrise.

Dennis began walking toward the front of the basement, toward the stairway leading up to the first floor. As he passed the offices, he looked inside. The accounting office was completely bare. Files and papers that had been tossed on the floor were no longer there. The safe was gone. The security office was also empty, completely devoid of furniture, and the video surveillance cameras were nowhere to be seen. Dennis hurried to the closet at the back of the room and opened the door. There was no blood, no sign of the dead security guard. Something had gone wrong. Nothing was the way it was supposed to be. He had waited too long. The sun was coming up. Dennis knew that there would be consequences if he didn't finish before sunrise. Now he would need to face those consequences.

***

Connor waited at the top of the steps leading down to the second floor and listened for any voices, footsteps, or any other sign that someone would be waiting for him on the next floor. No sounds were coming up the stairs. Slowly, quietly he moved down the stairs. The staircase went down seven steps and then flattened out on a small landing before continuing down another seven steps in the opposite direction. When he reached the landing, Connor stopped again to listen for any voices. He looked around the corner toward the bottom of the stairs but did not see anything, and he did not hear anything, so he proceeded down.

When he reached the second floor, he stopped. That was where he heard a sound, but he couldn't make out what it was or where it was coming from. Could it be Dennis? he wondered. He looked at the wall where the elevator would normally be. It was not there. The wall was bare. And just like the floor above, the second floor was completely devoid of everything. This was the floor that contained women's fashions and jewelry. All the merchandise, counters and advertising were there just a few hours earlier when he swept the floor. Now there was nothing. Even the shelving and display cases had been removed. As it was on the third floor, the wood floors on the second floor were scratched, warped, and dirty. They looked like they hadn't been touched in years. But that was impossible. Connor had just cleaned the floor earlier that evening. He had been cleaning and waxing that floor every Saturday night for two years. And every Saturday night, the floor was packed with merchandise. The display cases were full. The floors were nearly spotless.

Nothing was the way it had been just a few hours earlier. The reality he saw now was not the reality he had seen earlier in the evening. The sun was coming up. The cleaning crew would be arriving any time now. Connor needed to get to the first floor. But the closer he got to the stairs leading down to the first floor, the louder the noise became. Someone or something was moving around on the floor below him. He could hear the sound of footsteps and people talking. Could it be the cleaning crew? It was about time for them to arrive. Or could it be someone else? Maybe even Dennis. He would know that Connor's only escape route would take him through the first floor.

No, Connor thought. From the voices he heard, there were several people on the first floor. It had to be the cleaning crew, he reasoned.

For just a little bit, a calm came over him. His heart rate, racing ever since he left the fourth floor, slowed, and his breathing returned to normal. He was just fifty feet from being safe. His nightmare was about to end. Once he made it to the cleaning crew, he would be safe.

The sun is coming up. Dennis retrieved the black duffle bag. He got what he came for and surely would have left before the sun came up and before the cleaning crew arrived, he reasoned. Fourteen steps down to the first floor. He was almost there.

Connor moved quickly down the first seven steps to the landing between the second and first floors, where he waited just a second. The voices were louder now. From just below him, he could make out a woman's voice and two men's voices. *The woman's voice must be Erlinda*, he told himself. She was a heavy-set black lady in her late forties — the crew leader. Erlinda unlocked the front door every Sunday morning and was the first face Connor, and the security guard saw. Erlinda always gave him a big smile and hug. She was a happy, grandmotherly-type woman. Connor didn't know much about her. He only saw her for a brief minute as he was exiting the door and she was coming in. He'd always wanted to find out more about her, to talk to her, but he just hadn't taken the time before.

The men he wasn't sure about. Erlinda often had a different crew with her. Sometimes women, sometimes men, sometimes both. She worked for an independent cleaning service, and Adler was just one of her many customers.

Connor's heart began to race as he descended the final seven steps to the first floor. He was nearly free, nearly safe from the strangers, safe from Dennis, and safe from the nightmares on the other side of the vent on the fourth floor. He got to the last step before reaching the first floor, and then he stopped suddenly. There was another voice, a voice that he recognized.

Dennis ascended the basement stairs up to the first floor, carrying the black duffle bag. The people that sent him into Adler a few hours earlier were waiting for him. He turned the corner, and they were there, three of them.

"Give me the duffle bag," a woman's voice said. "Did you get the red jewelry box?"

"No. The boy took the gold key out of it. He has the key with him."

Connor recognized the voice of the woman. He knew her. He had heard her voice before. But he couldn't believe it was her voice. Connor quietly stepped down off the last step and peeped around the corner. He couldn't believe his eyes. *Maybe I am losing my mind*, he thought. Standing just a few feet from the front door was Linda Adler. Next to her were two large men. Dennis was also there, looking concerned and nervous.

"You mean the boy is still alive?" she asked in an agitated tone.

"Yes, but I can find him. He's somewhere on the second or third floor. He's got the gold key. Give me thirty minutes, and I'll find him and the key," Dennis said.

"No," she said sternly. "Our time is up. We have to proceed with our plan. You've disappointed me, Dennis." Then, she turned to the two men standing next to her, Anthony and Antonio Civelli. "More importantly, you've disappointed the Civelli family. I gave them my word that they could trust you to do the job. They depended on you, and you let them down. Tell me, Dennis, that you will be able to finish the rest of our plan without any more mistakes."

"Yes, I can," Dennis said.

"Then take the gasoline cans and soak down every inch of the first floor," Linda Adler said.

Connor hadn't noticed the gasoline cans, five in total, sitting on the floor just a few feet from the people. His eyes had been focused on the four people in the room. He also hadn't noticed that the first floor was completely bare, just like the second and third floors. Everything had been removed. Even the elaborate Christmas displays that were in the front windows that ran the length of the Adler building were gone. *They were there just three hours ago,* he thought to himself. *How could they disappear so quickly?*

Dennis began emptying the gasoline cans on the bare, wood floor. He started at the far end of the room and worked his way backward toward the front door. Linda stood just inside the front door, watching him. The two Civelli brothers took the steps down to the basement and disappeared from Connor's sight.

Connor quietly climbed the steps to the second floor. There was no way he would be able to exit from the first floor now. His only hope was to go back to the fourth floor and crawl through the vent to the hidden room, then take the steps up to the roof and escape down the fire escape.

When he reached the second floor, the fumes from the gasoline had already worked their way up to him. He knew now what their plan was. They were going to burn down the store. They had taken out every bit of merchandise, and now they were going to set fire to the store. *But, why*? he thought. *Why would Linda Adler steal from her own store and then burn it down*?

The answers to those questions came to him through his grandfather or something that appeared to be his grandfather. His image appeared just a few feet away from him without warning. His grandfather's image was not clear, as it had been when he saw him on the fourth floor. The image was foggy and weak. He could see right through his grandfather to the other side of the wall. He appeared like a soft cloud, one that would be seen on a sunny day. Parts of him were visible. Other parts were shallow, allowing the landscape behind to show through.

"Linda Adler owes her soul to the men downstairs. She sold herself to save her store. She would have lost it many years ago if it wasn't for those men. Dennis helped her. He had to. He owes his soul to those same men. They have come here tonight to collect. No one in this store is supposed to survive tonight. That's why I am here. I am going to correct your fate. But you must listen carefully to everything I tell you, and you must do exactly what I say. Do you understand?"

"No, I don't understand, Grandpa. None of this makes any sense. But I do trust you, and I'll do exactly what you tell me to do."

***

Dennis emptied all five gasoline cans, pouring the fuel on nearly every inch of the first floor. "Do you want me to start the fire?" he asked his mother.

"No, not yet," Linda told him. "The Civelli brothers are taking care of something in the basement. We'll wait for them."

Just as she said that, the Civelli brothers came up the stairs from the basement. "We need to hurry," Anthony yelled as he ran up the stairs.

Together, the group moved quickly to the storage room on the first floor. They had planned to exit the building from the dock door. The truck would be parked there, and they would load the duffle bag on the truck and drive away. That was the plan. Anthony Civelli pulled out part of a newspaper that he had stuffed in his coat pocket, then pulled out a book of matches that were in the same pocket. He struck a match, lit the newspaper on fire, and tossed the newspaper into the showroom. The flames exploded, quickly moving throughout the first floor until the entire floor was engulfed in a wall of flames.

***

Connor smelled the smoke before he saw the flames. But the smell of smoke wasn't just coming from the first floor. It was also coming from the back of the storage room. It was coming from the hidden stairway. They had set the stairs on fire too. *They were eliminating all escape routes from the store. They didn't plan for any witnesses to escape the fire.*

***

Dennis Morgan turned to exit the building. That's when he heard the gunshot, followed by tremendous pain. The pain shot through his lower back, up his spine, through his shoulders, and finally into his legs. Dennis fell like a rock. Fear gripped him when he realized what had happened. For most of his life, he had felt that this would be how his life would end. He didn't know when, he didn't know how it would happen, but he knew that it would, someday. The boy had often wondered how painful it would be to die and had hoped it would be quick and painless. It wasn't. The pain was greater than he thought anyone could bear. He prayed for it to end, or at least for him to pass out, but neither happened. Dennis watched as his mother left him on the floor, dying. Then he watched as she and the two men left the building through the dock door. He couldn't move. His spine had been shattered from the impact of the bullet, and he lay helplessly on the floor, watching the flames sizzle around him. The heat was intense. The smoke was dense. Dennis had never prayed before this day. But he prayed now that the smoke would take his life before the flames. His prayer went unanswered. Dennis smelled his flesh burning before he felt the pain.

***

Connor heard his screams from the second floor. He could not help him.

The smoke and heat had moved to the second floor now. Soon, the flames would reach Connor. His grandfather took his hand. "It will be all right. It is not your time," he told his grandson.

Suddenly, behind him, the elevator appeared where the wall had been. It opened. His grandfather motioned for him to get in the elevator. Dense smoke was now covering the entire second floor. Connor could see the flames shooting up the stairs from the first floor and could see the floor buckling. There was no time to lose. Connor got on the elevator. The smoke was so dense inside it that he had to hold his breath.

"Do you have the gold key?" his grandfather asked him.

"Yes," Connor said as he pulled the key out of his pocket.

"Use it. It will take you to the fourth floor. From there, you are on your own."

Connor put the key in the slot, turned it, and pressed the fourth-floor button. The door closed, and the elevator began climbing. Dark, thick smoke entered the elevator's shaft and blanketed Connor until he could no longer see inside the elevator. The smell of fire was everywhere. He held his breath as the elevator slowly moved upward. From the slight opening in the door, he could see flames. The fire had engulfed the elevator shaft. He heard the crackling sound of the fire. The cables pulling the elevator were making strange noises as if they were ready to break. Slowly the elevator continued upward. The air was impossible to breathe now. Connor struggled to hold his breath, one-minute, then two-minutes. Suddenly, the elevator stopped. That's when panic set in. His mind told him *The elevator is stuck. The flames are going to consume you. You're going to die trapped in this elevator.*

Just when he knew he couldn't hold his breath any longer and he was about to succumb to the smoke and flames, the elevator door opened up.

He exited quickly, taking a deep breath as soon as he got away from the smoke. Then he heard the sound, a loud moaning sound, followed by a boom. He turned back toward the elevator just as it plummeted to the floors below. The cables had given way, lasting just long enough to carry Connor to the fourth floor.

He took several deep breaths and moved into the center of the room. The smoke was thick — not as dense as it had been inside the elevator, but thick enough that it was hard to breathe. He took short, shallow breaths as he made his way through the showroom. Like he had seen on the second floor, the wood was starting to bow. The heat underneath had intensified. It would not be long before the entire floor gave way.

When he got to the door leading to the storage room, he could see the flames. The fire in the hidden stairway had moved all the way up the stairs and was billowing through the back walls and into the storeroom. Connor had no choice. This was the way to his only exit. He could hear sirens. The fire department was on the way. But he couldn't wait. They would not arrive soon enough to save him.

So, he took his shirt off, put it over his face to provide some air between his face and the shirt, and ran. He sprinted, much like he had often done during the last lap of one of his races. But this time, he wasn't running for a medal. This time he was running for his life. He could not see because of the dense smoke and flames, so he used his memory to guide him into the bedroom and to the vent. When he grabbed the vent screen, it was hot. He pulled it off and entered the vent. The aluminum walls of the vent were hot as well, burning his knees and arms as he worked his way through to the other side.

When he got to the hidden room, flames had burned through one of the walls. The heat was intense. He held on tightly to the shirt covering his face and ran as fast as he could through the flames. When he got to the steps leading to the roof, he felt the pain. His shirt was on fire, parts of it burning into his face. He threw it off him and ran up the steps. Three steps from the door exiting onto the roof, the stairs gave way, and Connor's left leg slipped underneath. He clung to the railing, desperately trying to gain his balance. When he was able to steady himself, he pulled the left foot onto the stair. The three steps in front of him were gone. He needed to jump, hoping he could reach the landing immediately in front of the door before the entire stairwell gave way.

Connor would need to jump off his right foot. The wound where the nail had penetrated his left foot was sore. Running through the showroom had aggravated it. It was too weak to put additional pressure on it. The boy would have only one opportunity to make a successful jump. The step he was standing on was bowing and about to give way. He bent his right knee, took a deep breath, and jumped just as the step below him gave way. The weight of his body fell short of the landing, catching the edge of it with his left foot and falling back. He grabbed the edge of the landing with his right hand as the rest of his body dangled off the edge. The only thing below him was flames.

He reached with his left hand to grab the landing just as his right hand was beginning to slide off. With both hands firmly on the edge of the landing, Connor used every bit of his arm strength to pull his body up to the landing. Once he was safe, he focused his attention on the door exiting to the roof. It was blocked. A large section of the wall to his right had collapsed just in front of the door. Connor tried to move it, but it was too heavy. He couldn't budge it. He was trapped. Connor couldn't go back, and he couldn't go forward. It was only a matter of minutes before the flames would reach him if the smoke didn't kill him first.

Connor had never been very religious. His parents were Lutheran, but they weren't very religious either. They forced Connor to go to Wednesday night bible study and Sunday church services, but they rarely went themselves. He had always thought there were a lot of hypocrites that went to church. They went there to feel good about themselves on Sundays but lived a less than Christian lifestyle the rest of the week. He never understood prayer. People prayed, and they would say that they talked to God, or God spoke to them. But the times Connor prayed, there was nothing but silence. God had never spoken to him. But Connor did believe in God. He believed in Heaven and hell. He believed in an afterlife.

So, for the first time in many years, he closed his eyes, bowed his head, and prayed. This time, God answered him. At least, God sent someone to answer him. His grandfather appeared in front of him, his image not clear, more like a hologram, floating in the air just above where the steps below him had been. "Everything will be okay, Connor. It is not your time," his grandfather said.

Then, like magic, the crumbled wall blocking his exit was lifted. The door opened, and Connor could see the roof. When he turned to his grandfather to thank him, he was gone. Connor got to his feet and ran onto the roof. Parts of it had already caved in. He could feel the heat of the fire through his shoes as he ran as fast as he could over the rooftop. Just as he reached the fire escape, a large section of the roof collapsed. He could see the lights of the fire trucks below as he climbed quickly down the fire escape. When he got to the bottom, two firemen carried him over to an ambulance and put an oxygen mask on him. Paramedics loaded him into an ambulance and drove away.

CHAPTER 16
THE HOSPITAL

Connor slept for nearly three days. He had second and third-degree burns on his lower legs, arms, and back. He had been sedated to alleviate some of the pain. When he woke, he had an IV attached to his arm, shooting a liquid substance into his vein. The room was dark, the shades to the window were closed, the lights were turned off. The room was small, cold, and ugly. The paint on the walls was peeling. Plaster had broken off in several spots. The floor was an old, worn linoleum. It was an ugly shade of gray with scuff marks embedded into the tiles. No one was in the room.

Where were his parents? He expected to see them in the room when he woke up. Maybe not his father, but at least his mother. Surely, she was worried about him. Maybe she stepped out to grab a cup of coffee or a bite to eat, or perhaps to talk to the doctor.

He was so tired. He could feel the drugs in his system. *It must be pain medication*, he thought. He didn't feel any pain. It must be working. He looked at his arms. They were both bandaged from his hands to his elbows. He pushed the cover off his legs. They were both bandaged, too, one from his foot to his knee, the other from his foot to his ankle. He must have been burned fleeing the building. Funny, with his adrenaline pumping, he had no idea that he got burned until now.

A buzzer went off, and a light flashed above the IV bag. It was empty. A nurse came into the room a few minutes later to replace the bag.

"Oh, you're awake, Mr. Allen," she said. "We were wondering when you would wake up. Can I get you any water? You must be thirsty."

"No, thanks. Where am I?" Connor asked.

"You're in a hospital, Mr. Allen. You suffered some rather serious burns. We are trying to help you," she said. "My name is Virginia Lighter. I'm your nurse."

Virginia was in her mid-to-late sixties but looked older, with piercing emerald-colored eyes. She wore almost no facial make-up except for lipstick. It was a bright rose-colored lipstick that seemed like an odd choice, given her pale complexion and green eyes.

"Nurse, where is my mother? Does she know I am here?"

"Yes, she knows, Mr. Allen. And she is quite worried about you, but she knows you need your rest right now. You will see her soon."

"What about Linda Adler and the people that started the fire? Did they catch them?"

"Mr. Allen, you need your rest. You've been through a lot. Please, try to sleep. The doctor will explain everything to you as soon as you're better."

Whatever drugs were in Connor's IV bag must have contained a strong sedative. Ten minutes after Nurse Lighter left, he was sound asleep. A week went by before he started to come out of the daze of the medication. He was groggy when he finally opened his eyes again, and he was in the same, dreary room, by himself. His mother was not there. There were no flowers, no cards, no sign that anyone had come into his room. His mother knew he was there. Nurse Lighter had told him so. She must have come in the room when he was asleep, he told himself. But why didn't she leave flowers, or a card, or a note, or something to let him know that she was there?

His bandages were off. His skin was a little red, but no noticeable scarring. His legs itched where the bandages had been. He pushed the bed sheet off so he could reach down and scratch the itch. That's when he noticed it. His right hand was handcuffed to the bed rail. He could not move it.

"What the hell is going on?" he said out loud. "Nurse Lighter," he yelled. There was no answer. "Nurse," he screamed as loud as he could. That got attention. Nurse Lighter and two male attendants rushed into the room.

"Mr. Allen, It's good to see that you are awake. But there is no need to scream. Some of the other patients are sensitive to loud noise. You must keep quiet. If you need me, there is a button hooked to your bed rail. Just push it, and I'll come in as quickly as I can."

"Where am I? Why am I handcuffed to the bed? What is going on?"

"The doctor will answer all your questions, Mr. Allen. But for now, you need to rest. You've been through a lot. Please lay back and relax. I'll have some food sent up right away. You have to be starving."

Then, one of the male orderlies handed her a needle. She wiped a vein on Connor's left arm with a sterile solution, then injected the needle into his arm. He tried to pull it out with his right arm, but the other orderly grabbed that arm and pulled it away.

"This will help you rest," Nurse Lighter said.

***

Janie Allen was not a strong woman. She had been rebellious in her youth, but those days were long gone. Her relationship with her husband, Ronald, had deteriorated over the years. They had talked about divorce more than once. He was a difficult, stubborn man that had been emotionally abusive to his wife for many years. That abuse had taken a toll on her. She was a shell of the person she used to be. He had isolated her from social interaction. She had no friends. The only people left in her life that she truly cared about were her mother, Rose, and her son, Connor.

Janie sat in her '64 Ford Falcon, with its rusty gray exterior and torn vinyl seats, and watched. There was nowhere else she wanted to be. She felt completely powerless, unable to see or talk to her son, unable to help or give him comfort, and unable to assure him that everything would be all right, even though she wasn't certain it would be. She wanted to see Connor, but she couldn't. It seemed Connor was the only thing good she had left in her life, and yet she had failed her son when he needed her the most. For quite some time now, they had drifted apart. He had isolated himself, and she had recognized that her son needed help but neglected to do anything about it. Now he was in trouble, and all she could do was sit in that parking lot, staring up at the tall, brick building that held her son, and hope for the best—hope that he got the treatment he needed, and hope that he would come home again.

His mother had been coming to that parking lot every day since he had been there. The first few days he was there, she tried to see him. She waited in the lobby. She talked to anyone that would listen. No one would tell her anything about her son. No one would let her see him. Finally, she was told to leave. "We will call you, Mrs. Allen, when we have news of your son," a nurse told her. Then, a security guard escorted her out the front door. "Please, don't come back until we contact you," the man said.

Since then, she had come to the parking lot every day. That was as close as she could get to her son. She looked at the cold, brick building, eight stories tall. She watched the windows, hoping to get a glimpse of her son, although she didn't even know what room he was in. She hoped, she prayed that he would come to the window, look out, and she would see him, and he would see her. She wanted so much to comfort him, to assure him that everything would be all right, even though she had no idea if it would. That asphalt parking lot was her second home. Her mother, Rose, had moved into her daughter's house temporarily. She was there to answer the phone in case the doctors called. Until they did, Rose would stay close to the phone, and Janie would spend her days in the parking lot looking at the windows, watching the people come and go, biding her time until she could see her son again.

Westminster Psychiatric Hospital had been an institution in Kansas City for over sixty years. The large, eight-story building had seen better days. The outside was weathered and in need of repair. The inside was cold, gray, and dark. The hallways were narrow. The rooms were small and plain. The heat that rose from the large boilers in the basement kept the upper levels too hot and the lower levels too cool. It made a loud racket when it turned on, and the noise billowed through the vents and pipes in the walls like a motorcycle engine on its last leg.

***

After three weeks, Connor was slowly weaned off his medication. He was taken out of his single room and placed in one with another occupant, room 713. His new roommate was a young man, just slightly older than Connor. He was skinny as a rail, with long, dark hair that was brushed back into a ponytail that ran down to the middle of his back. His roommate never talked. He made noises, mostly at night, mostly loud, and mostly screams. The noises were unprovoked and happened for no discernable reason. He laid in bed with his mouth open and stared into space most of the time. Sometimes he would turn his head and stare for hours at a time at Connor. He seldom blinked his eyes. He seldom altered his focus. He just stared. At mealtime, his food needed to be liquified in a blender before being served. It looked like baby food. He couldn't or wouldn't feed himself, so a nurse had to do it. He often had difficulty swallowing the food, so he would spit most of it back up, and it would run down his face.

The odor coming from his bed was horrendous. The staff rarely bathed him, and since he had no control of his bowel movements, the stink was terrible. He laid in his feces for hours at a time until someone came in to change him. Like Connor, his roommate had one hand cuffed to the bed rail.

Since Connor had one hand chained if he needed to go to the bathroom, he had to press the nurse's button, and that didn't always get someone to respond. He asked the nurses repeatedly about the handcuff that chained him to the bed? "Why am I here? When can I go home? Why am I locked to this bed?" The only response he ever got from the nurses was, "The doctor will talk to you as soon as you are better."

The thing was, he was better. His wounds no longer hurt. Since the medication was stopped, he felt more alert and more like himself. He was ready to go home. He was ready to see his mother and his father, and his grandmother. They had promised to send him home by Christmas, but now Christmas had come and gone. He was ready to go back to school. He was ready to get back to the normalcy of life. But they were treating him like a prisoner. Why hadn't his mother visited him? Why did the windows have bars on them? What kind of hospital was this? Why hadn't he seen the doctor yet? The nurses said that he would answer all his questions, but he hadn't even seen him yet. All those questions kept swirling through his mind.

The nurses and the other staff members that came into his room were of no help. They refused to answer any of his questions.

Nearly three weeks into his stay at Westminster, a nurse by the name of Erma Schmidt and two male orderlies entered his room. He had seen Nurse Schmidt many times before. She worked the day shift. When Nurse Lighter wasn't working, she would take care of him. The orderlies he remembered too. They were large men with angry looks. *They looked more like bouncers at a dive bar than orderlies in a hospital*, Connor thought. One of the male orderlies removed the handcuff from his left hand. The other lifted him out of bed and placed him in a wheelchair. Nurse Schmidt wheeled him out of the room with the two orderlies walking a few steps behind. She rolled him down the narrow hallway of the seventh floor. It was the first time he had seen that narrow, dark hallway. The only trip he had ever made was from one room to another, and that was done late at night when he was still under the influence of the medication.

Connor was wheeled into a small elevator, and an orderly pushed the button to the fourth floor. The elevator was slow and made a loud grinding noise as it maneuvered its way down. When the elevator reached the fourth floor, and the door opened, he was pushed down the hallway. The fourth floor looked identical to the eighth floor. The hallways were narrow, the lighting was poor, and the tile floor and walls looked in need of repair. He did notice one difference, though. When he got fifty feet down the hallway, there was a solid, steel door with a security guard sitting just before it. When the nurse got to the security guard, she showed him a badge, he pressed a button, and the steel door opened. Inside that area and on both sides of the corridor were offices, most containing names of doctors hanging from a sign on the doors.

The wheelchair stopped at the office of Dr. Benjamin Jacobs. The nurse pressed a button on the outside of the door, waited for a few seconds, and a tall, heavyset man in a white doctor's coat opened the door.

He held out his hand and said, "Hello, Connor. My name is Dr. Jacobs. It's good to finally meet you," he said as he shook Connor's hand. "Come in."

The nurse wheeled Connor to a seat just across from a large, oak desk.

"Please, Connor. Take a seat. Can you stand, or do you need help?"

Connor stood, sat down in the chair, and watched as the

nurse and the two orderlies left the room. "We'll be just outside if you need us, Doctor," one of the orderlies said as he shut the door.

Connor turned his attention to the doctor as he took a seat in a large, leather chair at his desk. "Can I get you a cup of coffee or a glass of water?" he asked.

"No. I'm fine. I just want to know what the hell is going on. Why am I here? Why was I handcuffed to the bed? Why hasn't my mother visited me?"

"Hold on," the doctor said. "I promise I will answer all of your questions. But first, I've got some questions of my own. Do you know where you are?"

"No."

"You're at Westminster Psychiatric Hospital. Do you remember coming here?"

"No. I remember being put in the ambulance, but I don't remember where they took me."

"That's understandable. You had some rather severe burns. The paramedics needed to sedate you."

"But why was I brought here?" Connor asked.

"The police thought it was the best place for you. Everyone was concerned about you. They just wanted to help you. They just wanted you to get well."

"I don't understand. Why wasn't I taken to a regular hospital?"

"Under the circumstances, this seemed like the best place for you to get the proper care you needed."

"Why handcuff me to the bed? Why hasn't anyone visited me? Does my mother even know I am here?"

"The handcuffs were a precaution. We didn't know how you would react when the sedatives wore off. Besides, we didn't want you to run off before we were able to help you," the doctor said with a hint of a smile on his face. "To answer your other questions, no one has visited you because you haven't been ready to see people yet. And yes, your parents know exactly where you are. They are both anxious to see you. But they know that it is important for you to get well first."

"I feel fine, Doctor. I don't understand why I can't see my mother."

"You've been through a lot, Connor. We've treated your burns. Physically, you are in good shape. But inside, you need some more time. Can you tell me about the night of the fire? Start with the very beginning of that night and provide me as much detail as you remember."

"Is that necessary, Doctor? I'd just as soon not relive that night. I was nearly murdered. It is something I would like to forget."

"I assure you, Connor, I need you to tell me everything that you remember from that night. I can't help you until you help me help you. You want to get better, don't you, Connor? You want to see your parents, don't you?"

"Yes."

"Then let's start with that night. Tell me everything you remember."

Connor told him everything he could remember about that night, starting with when he arrived for work.

"It was just Old Man Collins, the security guard, and me working that night. I started sweeping the floors like I started every Saturday night. When I finished sweeping, I went downstairs to get the floor waxing machine. I was about to start waxing the floors downstairs when I saw Bill Collins run up the stairs. He never ran. I knew something was wrong, so I went into the security office. They have monitors in there that show every part of the store, wherever there is a security camera. I looked on the monitors until I saw Bill Collins. Four men were coming into the store through the back door. I saw Bill struggle with the men and fall to the ground. Then I saw the men dragging him. That's when I got scared. I ran into the basement and hid behind the mannequins. I saw the men drag Bill down the stairs into the security office. I saw one of the men put a gun to his head and shoot him. Then they put his body in the closet. Two of the men went back upstairs while the other two men stayed in the basement. One of the men turned off the breaker switch, and the building went dark. Then one man went into the security room while the other went into the accounting office. The man in the accounting office opened the safe and removed everything inside, and put the items in a black duffle bag. Soon, the other man finished in the security office and went upstairs. That's when I tried to find a better hiding place. Unfortunately, I stepped on a nail, knocked some boxes over, and the man that was downstairs heard me. When he found me, I struggled with him but was able to stab him in the neck with the nail that I had pulled out of my foot. Are you sure that you want to hear everything?"

"Yes, please continue."

"Well, I thought that I had killed the man, so I went to the security room to see if I could help Bill. I found him in the closet. He was barely breathing. There was nothing that I could do. The door to the accounting office was open. I saw the duffle bag laying on the floor. It had the money from the safe in it. I picked it up and took it with me. I don't know why. I guess that I thought it would buy me some time. The money would give me a bargaining chip that I might be able to use to stay alive. I took the bag and headed for the hidden stairway in the back of the basement. Bill had told me about it. All that I could think about was that I needed to get out of the basement. Bill had told me that the hidden stairway would lead up to the other floors without needing to use the front stairs or the freight elevator. I knew that the men would see or hear me if I went either of those ways.

"On the way to the stairway, I went right by the area where I had stabbed the stranger. But his body was gone. I was sure then that he had survived the stab wound and would be looking for me or alerting the other men, so I rushed to the back stairway. That's when the stranger that I had stabbed caught up to me. We struggled. He grabbed the gun that I had taken from him during the first struggle and pointed it at me. I was sure he would kill me. But a shelf fell on him, and a knife from that shelf fell and stabbed him. He was dead.

"Now, I know that you are going to think this is crazy, Doctor, but I could have sworn that I saw my grandfather push the shelf over on the man. He saved my life. But the strangest part is, my grandfather died over twelve years ago."

Doctor Jacobs took notes, and when Connor stopped talking, waiting for some type of reaction from the doctor, he said, "Please continue."

"Then, I hid the body under the stairwell and started up the stairs. There were no exit doors leading to the other floors until I got to the fourth floor. That floor is where I spent most of the night. I met a man named David Morgan on that floor. He wasn't exactly happy to see me. He clobbered me over the head and tied me to a bed."

"Bed? Where was the bed?" the doctor asked.

"The bed was in a room in the storage room portion of the fourth floor. According to David Morgan, it used to be an office. Thomas Adler, many years earlier, converted it to a bedroom so he could sleep there nights when he was too tired to go home."

"I assume Thomas Adler was Linda Adler's father, and he converted the office when he managed the store many years earlier. Is that correct?"

"Yes."

"Okay, now who is David Morgan?"

"He was Linda Adler's husband years ago. But they have been divorced for some time."

"I see. And what was he doing on the fourth floor?"

"He told me that he had been destitute. He had squandered all his money and was living on the streets when Bill found him and brought him to Adler. He put him up on the fourth floor, which hadn't been used for years. It had a bed and kept him off the streets and out of the cold."

"How did Bill Collins know David Morgan? And why did he decide to help him?"

"I don't know all the details. I know that they had met while David was still married to Linda Adler. I can tell you what he told me, but I really don't think it pertains to what happened that night, Doctor."

"Never mind, we can discuss that some other time. Go on."

"David Morgan tied me to the bed and took the black duffle bag with the money. It turned out that his son, Dennis, was one of the strangers that broke into the store. It also turned out that David knew about the break-in. He was part of it. But he was scared. He didn't know about the others. He thought that only his son and Bill were going to be involved in the break-in. When he heard the gunshots and the other strangers, he knew something had gone wrong with the plan. He was afraid that his son had been killed. He wanted my help to hide or escape if it became necessary. That's when I became aware of the other people on the fourth floor."

"What people? Tell me about them."

"You will find this hard to believe, Doctor. I certainly did. But the other people that occupied the fourth floor were ghosts. My grandfather was one of them, one of the good ghosts who occupied the showroom on the fourth floor. They said they were there to correct fates, to help lost souls find their way. They said someone intended to change my fate, and they were there to protect me. But they didn't like David Morgan. They wouldn't allow him to come into the showroom. David asked for my help in convincing the ghosts to let him in if he needed to hide from the strangers.

"The strange thing was that there was another way out of the building. There was a vent in the bedroom that led to a hidden room behind the wall. The hidden room led to a stairway that went up to the roof. David could have taken that stairway to the roof, and from there climbed down the fire escape to the street below. I could have done the same. But neither of us had the nerve to try to escape that way."

"Why? That would seem like your best, most logical option."

"There was something terrifying on the other side of that vent, living in the hidden room behind the walls. They made horrible noises. They had attacked David before. He called them 'bad ghosts.' My grandfather warned me about them. He said that he couldn't protect me if I went into that room. So, neither of us tried to escape that way. We hoped the good ghosts would protect us. But, they would only help me. They refused to help him. David had done something horrible in that room, years earlier. That was one of the reasons the good ghosts were in that room. They were there to guide his lost soul to where it belonged."

"What had he done? "the doctor asked.

"David murdered Thomas Adler many years earlier. Mr. Adler was one of the ghosts in that room. David was also involved in a triple murder. He was caught having an affair in that room with my grandfather's wife. My grandfather was murdered, along with his wife."

"Wait, you said it was a triple-murder. Who was the third victim?"

"It was David Morgan."

"You mean it was a murder-suicide?"

"No. Bill Collins shot all three of them."

"Why? And how did Bill Collins get involved?"

"Bill was sent by Linda Adler. He was doing what was asked of him. Linda was behind everything. She was the mastermind of the robbery that night. She and two men that I had never seen before started the fire. I think they were members of the mob, the Civelli family. I don't know why the mob was involved. Maybe she was in debt to them, maybe she owed them. It doesn't matter. They were involved in the plan to steal from Adler and burn the building down. They also murdered Dennis Morgan. I saw them."

"What happened to David? And what happened to his son and the other two men that broke into the store with him?"

"Dennis shot the two men that helped him break into Adler. He shot them on the stairs leading up to the fourth floor. They died. David watched his son kill them. Maybe that was part of the plan all along, I don't know. After he shot the men, Dennis and David Morgan came into the fourth floor. They were looking for me, and they were looking for a red jewelry box containing a gold key. It was on some list that Dennis had. He was instructed by Linda Adler to kill me and get that key. They came into the showroom looking for me. The ghosts let them in. That's when the room changed. That's when it got dark in the room. That's when the scene in the room changed to the night that David Morgan was killed. My grandfather was there. So was his wife. So was Bill Collins. He killed all three of them. He shot them dead right in that room."

"Wait, slow down. You said David Morgan was killed that night?

"Yes, that's right."

"But you also said he was watching inside the room when it happened?"

"Yes, that's right. As crazy as it sounds, David was standing next to his son, watching the triple-murder occur right in front of him. He watched his own murder take place. Then, he just disappeared."

"Disappeared? How do you explain that?"

"I think his soul went where it was supposed to go. I think the people in that room were there to help him correct his fate, to help his soul go wherever it was supposed to go."

"What did Dennis do when his father just seemed to

vanish?"

"He came looking for me and the duffle bag. I was hiding inside the vent, ready to run to the hidden room if I had to. I was running out of options. I was afraid of what was on the other side of the vent, but I had no other way to escape. I heard the ghosts. I knew they were waiting. I knew they were angry. But with Dennis standing between me and the door to the showroom, I had no other way out. When he opened the vent and saw me, I tossed the duffle bag through the vent and into the hidden room. Then I tried to escape that way. But he caught me by the legs and pulled me out. I was able to get free and run into the showroom. I hoped that the ghosts would protect me. Dennis decided to go after the duffle bag before he came after me. The ghosts in the hidden room nearly killed him.

"Once he got the duffle bag, he came after me. I was standing at the far end of the showroom with my grandfather — or his ghost, I suppose. He handed me the gold key, the one that was inside the jewelry box, the one that Dennis was looking for. He told me to use it to travel down the elevator to another floor, a safe floor. I looked around. There was no elevator. But as soon as he handed me the key, an elevator appeared directly behind me. I got inside it and turned the key. The door started to shut, but Dennis Morgan got his hand inside the door just before it closed. That was the second time I thought he was going to kill me. But the ghosts saved me. They pulled him away from me, the elevator door shut, and I started down. I wanted to go all the way to the first floor. That was my plan. I would get out of the elevator and run for the front door or the door leading to the dock and escape.

"But the elevator had a mind of its own. It stopped on the third floor and wouldn't go any further. I got out and started walking down the steps. The weird thing was that the floors, all of them, were completely empty. I had just been on each of them earlier in the evening sweeping the floors. The counters, cash registers, merchandise, everything was there earlier in the evening. But now the floors were completely empty. They looked like they had been vacant for a long time…years.

"When I got a few feet away from the first floor, I heard voices. At first, I thought it was the cleaning crew. The sun was about to come up, and they usually showed up at the store about that time. But then I recognized one of the voices. It was Linda Adler. I waited at the stairway, out of sight. Then I heard Dennis Morgan. He had gone down the rear staircase and was now talking to Linda Adler and two other men. I heard him tell them that I was still alive and that I had the gold key. But I didn't have the gold key — I left it in the elevator. Now the elevator was gone. I knew they would come looking for me. I knew they would try to kill me. Then I saw the gasoline cans sitting on the floor next to the men. They picked up the cans and started coming toward me. I heard Linda Adler tell them to cover the floor with gasoline. That's when I moved up the stairs to the second floor. I didn't want to be spotted. But I didn't want to get too far away in case I had an opportunity to get out of the store through the first floor. I thought that if they started a fire, they would leave right after it started. That might give me enough time to get to the storage room on the first floor and out through the exit door at the dock before the fire spread too far.

"Then I smelled the smoke, but it wasn't coming from the front of the store where they had poured the gasoline. It was coming from the hidden stairway leading from the basement to the fourth floor. Someone must have set the stairway on fire. A few minutes later, the fire started on the first floor. I heard the people in the storeroom on the first floor. I assumed they were going to escape through the dock door, the same way the strangers entered the store early in the evening. But when I heard a gunshot, I knew they had other plans. They shot Dennis Morgan. I knew that when I heard him screaming as the flames reached him. It was too late for me to try to escape through the first floor. The flames were too hot, and the smoke was too dense. That was when the elevator reappeared. That was also when I saw my grandfather for the last time. He told me to take the elevator to the fourth floor. He told me to escape through the vent and up the rear stairs to the ceiling. He told me that everything would be all right. He told me that it wasn't my time.

"That's what happened the night of the fire. Linda Adler was responsible for the fire. She was responsible for the murders and the robbery. Have the police found her, or the two men that were with her?"

"That is a discussion we will have at another time," the doctor said. "I think that's about all the time we have today. You need your rest, and I need to digest what you just told me. We'll take this conversation back up in a couple of days. You and I have a lot to talk about."

Dr. Jacobs pushed a button on his desk, and two orderlies stepped inside the office. "Anthony and Antonio, will you please take Mr. Allen back to his room?" One pushed the wheelchair over to Connor and helped him into it.

"Wait, Doctor. Can I go home now? Can I see my mother?"

"I'm afraid we need a little more time, Connor. You will be here for a while."

As the two orderlies pushed him down the narrow, dark hallway of the fourth floor, Connor didn't notice the detective waiting just outside the doctor's office. Detective Roger Horning watched Connor roll down the hallway, stopping at the security door, and then down the outer hallway to the elevator. When he was out of sight, the detective knocked on Doctor Jacobs's door. The door opened, and he walked in and sat down in the chair across from the doctor.

Before Dr. Jacobs acknowledged the detective, he pressed a button on his desk. His secretary walked in. "Ms. Caldwell, would you mind asking Dr. Collins to step in here, please?"

"Yes, sir. I'll get him."

"Thank you, Denise," he said. "Detective, I think it is best if Dr. Collins joins us. Do you mind?"

"No, not at all. Under the circumstances, I think that is a good idea."

A few seconds later, the door opened, and Dr. Collins stepped in.

"Thank you for joining us, Bill. Detective, Dr. Collins was Connor's psychiatrist before his escape. He had treated Connor ever since he arrived at Westminster several years ago. I think it important that he be present."

"I completely agree. Dr. Collins, may I ask why Connor was admitted here?"

"Connor first came here nearly twelve years ago. He had suffered a traumatic brain injury after a near-drowning. He was in a coma for over a year. When he came out of it, he had a psychotic breakdown. He heard voices in his head. He developed a multiple personality disorder. At first, there was only one other personality. That was his grandfather. His grandfather was the one that found him in the water. His grandfather was the one that gave him CPR and brought him back to life. When his personality first began to split, his grandfather would only appear once in a while, usually at night, and only for short periods of time. But then other personalities began to show up. He had three roommates when he first arrived at Westminster. He called them Pole, Mouse, and Steam Pipe. Each were short-term patients. Over a two-week period, all had been discharged. But then, one by one, they began to appear in Connor's personality.

"I treated him with medication. We met three times every week. With time, he began to improve, so much so that we planned on releasing him on Christmas Eve. His mother had planned a huge celebration for him. It would have been the first Christmas he had been home in twelve years. Just two days before he was scheduled to be released, we moved a new roommate into his room. He was a young man, just a few years older than

Connor. He had deteriorated during his time at Westminster and no longer talked. He had to be force-fed. He had become a shell of a person. I thought that putting him in the room with Connor would benefit both of them. I thought, somehow, they might communicate with each other. They might give each other a reason to get better. That person was Dennis Morgan. At the time, I didn't know he was part of the Adler family. As far as I knew, he had been a patient at Westminster for a long time. He had serious mental problems that had manifested into a deep depression. He had stopped eating and seemed to have given up on life. I thought having a roommate about his age that had come through similar challenges and was vastly better now might give him a reason to live, to improve his mental state. In hindsight, it was a mistake."

"Thank you, Dr. Collins, for that information," the detective said. Then he turned his attention to Dr. Jacobs. "Dr. Jacobs, did Connor shed any light on why he burned down the Adler building?"

"No, I'm afraid not. He is still delusional. His mind believes that Linda Adler was responsible for burning down the building."

"So, he doesn't know that Mrs. Adler has been dead for over ten years?"

"No. He believes he worked in Adler every Saturday night for two years, sweeping and waxing the floors. His personalities are split equally between himself and his grandfather now. They are intertwined in such a way that he cannot distinguish between his actions and his grandfather's actions. He completely believes that he once worked at Adler, just as he believes he was a star athlete, a long-distance runner. His grandfather was the one that worked at Adler, sweeping and waxing floors. His grandfather was the one that ran track and cross country. But in his mind, he completely believes that he did those things. He said he was there, at Adler, working the night of the fire. He said there was a robbery that night, that a man named Bill Collins, a security guard at Adler, was murdered. He told an incredible story about a robbery, ghosts, a person living on the fourth floor by the name of David Morgan, and the murder of his son, a man named Dennis Morgan, who was part of a gang of four that killed Bill Collins and robbed the store. The fact is that he truly believes that story. In my opinion, he can no longer distinguish between reality and fiction. His mind has entered a realm where his imagination has taken control of any rational thought.

"Detective, do any of those names I just mentioned mean anything to you? Is there any possibility that there could be even a grain of truth in his story?"

"Yes, the names are familiar to me. Linda Adler, David Morgan, along with an elderly man and his wife named Ron and Denise Caldwell, were murdered over ten years ago on the fourth floor of Adler. The murders were sensational news. The strange part is, and you'll get a kick out of this, Doctor, a man named Bill Collins was arrested for the murders. You must remember something about them, Doctor."

"Yes, I didn't live in Kansas City at that time, but I remember the story made the national news. It was on all the major television networks. Wasn't it some sort of love triangle?"

"Yes, that's right. David Caldwell was having an affair with a married woman that worked at Adler. He was married to Linda Adler, the owner of Adler department store. Mrs. Adler suspected her husband of cheating. He had always been a bit of a scoundrel. She hired an ex-member of the Kansas City police force named Bill Collins to follow them and gather evidence of an affair. Bill was a bit of a scoundrel in his own right. He was rumored to have ties to the mob. He got in pretty deep with them after his wife died. She had cancer. The hospital bills and treatments were more than he could handle. Some say he turned to the mob for money to treat her and keep her alive as long as possible. There is a theory that everything that happened that night was the result of what happened to his wife. She used to be a sales associate on the fourth floor of Adler. Doctors suspected that her cancer was the result of being exposed to asbestos. The walls and ceiling on the fourth floor were full of it. Mrs. Adler knew about it, but it was too costly to replace, so she left it there. After his wife died, Bill went off the deep end. He quit the police force and started drinking heavily. He took a job as a security guard at Adler a short time later. Either he had some dirt on Mrs. Adler, or she just felt sorry for him, but either way, she hired him. It wasn't long after that she asked him to follow her husband.

"He was following him the night of the murders. Some think he called Linda Adler when he saw her husband and his lover go into Adler. Then, some say, he called Ron Caldwell — or perhaps he was working both sides of the fence, spying for both Linda Adler and Ron Caldwell. Whatever he was doing, they both showed up that night at Adler. They both went up to the fourth floor in the elevator. That's when the details of what happened get a little fuzzy. We know that Bill Collins killed everyone. He confessed to that. But we don't know if he intended to kill everyone or if he hoped that the jealous husband and the jealous wife would do it for him. We know that both Mrs. Adler and Ron Caldwell had guns on their persons that night. But they were never fired. According to Bill Collins, he murdered all four of them. Then he called his mob buddies, the Civelli brothers. They showed up on the fourth floor a little bit later with several cans of gasoline. We think they intended to set fire to the fourth floor, maybe to cover up the murders.

"When the police found the bodies the next morning, gasoline had been poured on all the victims except Bill Collins and the two Civelli brothers. Bill confessed to killing them too. That was his plan for getting out of the control of the mob. He intended to set fire to the place and then escape. He may have gotten away with it, too, if it wasn't for an elevator key. The key unlocked the elevator and allowed it to go between floors. Bill never could find that key. It was in the elevator when he, and then the Civelli brothers, used it to come up to the fourth floor. But somehow, it disappeared. He said that he checked all the bodies and every inch of the elevator and fourth floor for that key, but it was nowhere to be found. At the time, he didn't know about the hidden stairway. He didn't know that there was any other way to get up or down from the fourth floor than that elevator. And the elevator wouldn't move without the key. He sat there and waited on the fourth floor with those bodies until the police arrived the next morning. Funny thing was that the police used that same elevator to get up to the fourth floor. They pressed the button, the door opened, and inside the elevator, the key was right where it was supposed to be, in the control panel of the elevator."

"Detective, what happened to Bill Collins?" Dr. Collins asked.

"He committed suicide three days after he was arrested. He hung himself in his cell at the county jail. I assume he is no relation to you, Dr. Collins?"

"No. No relation."

"By the way, Doctor, how is Dennis Morgan doing? Any improvement?"

"No, I'm afraid not. He hasn't spoken a word in nearly two years. Did you recover all the bodies, Detective?"

"We think so, but there is no way of knowing for sure. He buried them all over the woods behind the Adler mansion. Some of the graves had washed away. Animals got to some of the bodies. We can never be sure that all his victims will be recovered."

"In all my years of psychiatry, I've never seen a more disturbed individual. His mind completely snapped after the death of his parents. It's a shame. He inherited everything from their estate. He could have lived comfortably the rest of his life. I wasn't at this hospital when they brought him in, but I heard it took six orderlies to tie him down and sedate him."

"Detective, were you there at the Adler mansion when they arrested him?"

"Yes."

"Did you go into that basement?"

"Yes."

"Was it as horrible as people said?"

"Worse, much worse. That's where we found him. I'll never forget what I saw that night as long as I live."

"Was it true about what he was wearing?"

"Yes. He skinned those poor boys alive, took their skins, and made them into a coat. He was wearing that coat the night we found him."

"How could he kill his friends that way?"

"They weren't friends. Dennis Morgan was not capable of having friends. They were victims. He selected them for slaughter. When he first set eyes on those boys, he knew that he would kill them. Linda Adler sent him to Westminster because she knew how sick he was. She knew what he was capable of. He should have never been released. I'm sorry, Dr. Collins. I didn't mean anything by that. I understand you were the one to discharge him."

"Yes, not my greatest moment. But he had me fooled. He had been an ideal patient. All signs were that he was cured. Instead, he preyed on the boys he knew from his time at Westminster, the ones that had been released. God only knows how many victims there actually were."

"That basement was the most gruesome crime scene I have ever seen. The walls were painted in blood. The smell was so bad we had to wear masks to stand it. And those dogs. There must have been two dozen of them. Most had to be shot just to get into the basement. The others were euthanized within a few days. Once you've given animals a taste of human flesh, they will turn into killers."

"Detective, why do you think he fed his victims to the

dogs?"

"We'll never know. My guess is that he got tired of burying his victims. So Doctor, what are you going to do with Connor Allen?"

"The boy needs a lot of help. I think he is going to be here for a long time."

"Doctor, why do you think he picked the Adler building to burn down? It never reopened after the murders over ten years ago. There was nothing there."

"That's one thing that I hope to find out. I suspect it has something to do with his grandfather, Ron Caldwell. He was one of the victims that night. Remember, his personality had split between his grandfather and himself. For all we know, it could have been Ron Caldwell that escaped and started the fire that night. Maybe it was some sort of revenge against the store where he died."

"Had he waited just a few days, that store would have been gone anyway. It was scheduled for demolition just after the first of the year," said the detective. "By the way, Doctor, did Connor mention anything about a gold key?"

"Yes, he did, several times. He claimed that his grandfather gave him the key to operate the elevator. Without it, he would have never been able to escape the flames. Why do you ask?"

"The fire investigators found a gold key laying on the floor of the old shaft that used to contain the elevator. They thought it was odd because every bit of the building had burned. The fire destroyed everything inside. But the key they found was undamaged. It looked brand new."

"Detective, did they happen to find a red jewelry box? Connor said that when his grandfather handed him the key, it was inside a red jewelry box. He said that jewelry box was on a list Dennis Morgan had of things he was looking for in Adler that night."

"No, there was no jewelry box. But I saw a red jewelry

box in the basement of the Adler mansion the night we arrested Dennis Morgan. It was on a workbench. It was open. Nothing was inside it. I remember Dennis insisted that he be able to take the jewelry box with him. He said something about needing to find the key that was supposed to be inside it. He said he needed to find the key to set the people free or something crazy like that."

"Doctor, which room is Dennis Morgan in?"

"I thought you knew, Detective. He's in room 813. He's sharing the room with Connor Allen. They were roommates before the escape, so after Connor's wounds healed, I thought it was best to put him back in a familiar situation."

"Doctor, I hope you have taken measures to keep him from escaping again."

"Yes, we have. He is handcuffed to the bed. The door is locked from the outside, and the windows to his room have bars on them. There is no way he'll escape again. The odd thing about his escape is that he was just a day away from being released. Had Connor waited one day, he would have been free. He went to all that trouble to set a fire. Now he is going to be here for a long time."

"Detective," Doctor Jacobs asked. "Do you know whatever happened to the Adler mansion?"

"Yes, that was a strange thing. Everyone assumed the city would need to tear it down. They put it up for public auction, and someone bought it. They fixed it up and are living in it now. You may have heard her name. She used to come here to visit her grandson. The mansion was purchased by Rose Caldwell."

-END-

Alan Brown grew up in the suburbs of Kansas City and graduated from Shawnee Mission East High School in 1973 and Avila University in 1979. Now He lives in a suburb of St. Louis, MO, with my wife and three daughters. He also has four sons that are grown and living outside the home. He enjoys writing about experiences he had growing up, examining the fantastical side, the dark side of a person's natural fears. All of his books are based on a reality in his life. He is a fan of Alfred Hitchcock. Like his stories, Alan Brown's will conclude with a twist, something he hopes will take the reader by surprise.

Made in the USA
Monee, IL
21 February 2021